DANGEROUS ENCOUNTER

DANGEROUS ENCOUNTER

Julie Coffin

CHIVERS

| British Library Cataloguing in Publication Data available |

This Large Print edition published by BBC Audiobooks Ltd, Bath, 2008.
Published by arrangement with the author.

U.K. Hardcover ISBN 978 1 405 64324 5
U.K. Softcover ISBN 978 1 405 64325 2

Printed and bound in Great Britain by
Antony Rowe Ltd., Chippenham, Wiltshire

CHAPTER ONE

I could see Jamie down by the water's edge, paddling through small rock pools left by the tide. Every so often he stopped, crouched down on his heels and peered into the shallow water, trailing his fingers.

I watched his fair head turn sideways, then nod, and realised he was talking to someone. But the beach was empty. No-one else was there. Only the two of us.

'Look, Mummy!'

He ran across the sand, his little face glowing with sunshine and excitement. His fingers uncurled.

'Matthew says it's a mermaid's purse.'

I looked at the dried brown object lying on his palm, and smiled.

'It's an egg case, Jamie. From a dog fish, I think.'

'I know it is really,' he said, stroking it with one finger. 'Matthew told me. When the baby fishes have come out, it floats to the shore.'

'Who's Matthew?' I asked casually.

'My friend,' he said, turning to scamper back to the pools again, sand flying out from under his bare feet.

Lots of children have imaginary friends, I reasoned. Especially only children. And after the turmoil of the divorce, it wasn't surprising that Jamie should invent one.

His whole world had been turned upside down. And his father moving to New Zealand with his new wife and her children devastated him. How can you explain that to a four-year-old? How could I reassure him that of course his daddy still loved him, when I knew only too well that he didn't? That he'd made a new life for himself and cast off the old one. My whole world had been turned upside down too.

So when my cousin, Sarah, suggested looking after her cottage in Cornwall, while she was working in America on a two-year contract, I said yes straight away. I needed a new life, too.

It seemed like a good idea. Or so I thought. But if I'd known, then, what was to come, would I have gone there?

Jamie settled in immediately, which surprised me. He was usually a bit wary about new places and events. But here it was different.

The cottage was almost on the beach, overshadowed by towering granite cliffs. A rather dark sort of place, with thick, white-washed, stone walls, thin grey slates and tiny deep-set windows. Gulls swirled and dipped from rocky ledges, their shrill cries echoing.

At night waves thundered against the cliffs, dragging shingle as they retreated with a long-drawn-out swish of sound. Everything in the cottage rattled or creaked or shook. But none

2

of that worried Jamie.

While I hardly slept, he went out like a light as soon as his head touched the pillow, and was up and eager for the beach as soon as daylight came. He talked non-stop about Matthew and what he said or did.

We'd been there for three weeks, and I still found it difficult to sleep. That night the air was humid and heavy, making it an effort even to breathe. Sheet lightning blazed far out to sea and there was an ominous rumble of thunder, growing nearer.

Then, from Jamie's room, I heard his voice murmuring. Guessing the storm had disturbed him too, I tiptoed in.

He was kneeling on his bed, gazing out of the window, his chin cupped between his hands. Not even flinching, as I did, with each thunder-clap and dazzling flash.

'We're watching for the ship, Mummy. Matthew says it be going to hit the rocks, then we can go down to the beach and gather in the treasure.'

'Oh, yes,' I teased, ruffling his soft fair hair, relieved to see he wasn't scared by the fury of the storm. 'And what sort of treasure will there be?'

He twisted his head sideways and I saw him nod, then turn back to me. 'Could be chests of gold coins and silver plate. Silken material, the like you never do see before, muslin and lace. Mebbe baccy and casks of brandy or rum

3

even.'

My body iced as I listened to the words. Words my small son would never know.

'Jamie,' I said, wrapping the duvet round him. 'You'd better come into my room until the storm is over.'

His body arched, his hands pushing me away.

'No!' he shrieked. 'I want to stay with Matthew and see the ship be wrecked.'

'Darling!' I protested, trying to hold him still. 'There's nothing out there.'

'There is! There is! Matthew says it be coming in fast. Look, Mummy.'

As he spoke, there was a tremendous crash of thunder and at the same time the whole sky seemed to explode into brightness. Through the rain-spattered window I saw the sea, lit as though it were day. Huge waves hurled, white-crested, against the cliffs, spiralling upwards into towering fountains of spray.

And sweeping in with them was a boat, mast splintered and twisted, heading straight towards the jagged outline of the rocks.

Momentarily, I closed my eyes, refusing to believe what I was seeing. But when I opened them again, the boat was still there, even closer, dipping and rising as each wave tore over it.

'Wait for me, Matthew!'

Jamie was clawing his way out of my enclosing arms, running to the bedroom door,

4

almost tumbling down the steep flight of wooden stairs in his haste.

I followed, snatching our anoraks from pegs in the hallway as I passed. Even before Jamie or I reached it, the cottage door leaned inwards, thudding against the wall, as though pushed by an unseen hand.

I knew it had to be the force of the gale and lashing rain, but still it terrified me.

'Jamie!' I cried out, seeing his small figure racing down the beach.

Sand swirled, swept by the wind, searing into my skin and eyes. My bare feet slipped and stumbled on rough shingle, my soaking nightdress tangling round my legs, almost tripping me. With every flash of lightning, the sea seemed to boil and the sound of it was terrible.

Then, above the clamour, came the sound of splintering wood and for a moment, silence, as if the elements were waiting.

'No, Matthew! No!'

I heard my son's anguished cry and then I was beside him, my arms enclosing his drenched little body, pulling him back from the drag of the sea.

Bits of wood flew high in the air, crashing down on to the sand and shingle with a shuddering thud. Lightning quivered around us as I knelt, holding my son, while he sobbed into my shoulder as if his heart was breaking. With the next flash of brilliance I saw a dark

5

shape swirl in towards the beach, then it was taken back again by the tug of the current.

'Don't move, Jamie!' I commanded, leaving him. 'Stay there.'

And as the next wave curled over, I reached out, feeling its strength snatch at my toes as they sank into the hidden sand.

My cold fingers clutched at cloth, my arms wrenching as the sea tried to tear it away from my grasp. Refusing to let go, I fought to keep my grip, my nails burying into the wet material.

Slowly and gradually, I hauled the heavy body up over the stones. And as the sky splintered into brightness once more, I saw it was a man, his face blood-streaked.

Jamie's cold, wet hand slipped into mine. 'Is he dead, Mummy?'

'I don't know, sweetheart,' I whispered.

'Shouldn't we breathe into him, like they do on the television?'

Should I, or force out the water first, I wondered? If only I knew the basics of First Aid. Should he be turned on his side? Wasn't that the correct thing to do?

But maybe he was already dead.

The man's body lurched and he gave a groan. From the noises that followed, I guessed he was bringing up swallowed water.

I crouched down beside him. 'Can you stand? Our cottage is farther up the beach. If you can make it there . . .'

He groaned again and I felt the shingle shift as he struggled to his knees. With an arm round my shoulders, he heaved himself slowly to his feet, almost pulling me over.

It seemed to take for ever to reach the cottage, stopping every metre or so for him to rest. His weight leaned into me and I tried not to stumble.

'Jamie, run on,' I urged. 'Get the towels from the bathroom and the duvets off our beds. Put them in the kitchen. We'll be there soon.'

Once inside, with the heavy wooden door closed and the kettle boiling, the sound of the storm didn't seem quite so fierce. The man hunched over the table, my pink bath towel swathed round him, rubbing his face and hair with another. He studied me with red-rimmed eyes and frowned.

'How did you manage to drag me out?' His voice was hoarse from the salt.

'From the sea, you mean?'

He shook his head and drops of water spattered the table. 'No, from the boat.'

'But I didn't. You were swept up on to the shore.'

He tugged at his soaking sweatshirt and pulled it over his head, and I saw that his body was lean and tanned, red weals already forming from his encounter with the rocks. When he began to struggle out of his jeans, I looked quickly away.

7

'Well, somebody did. I remember being below deck, trying to re-start the engine, when it struck the rocks. It was pitch-dark. Then I'm sure someone grabbed my arms and dragged me out.'

His deep-set blue eyes scanned my face. 'It wasn't you?'

I shook my head.

Tugging at my sleeve, Jamie whispered in my ear. 'It was Matthew, Mummy.'

Ignoring him, I put teabags into two mugs, added boiling water and milk, then passed one to the man.

'Well, whatever happened, you're safe and that's all that matters. I'm Becca and this is my son, Jamie.'

I looked at him, waiting for his name in return.

With both hands gripping the sides of the mug, he sipped the tea, his eyes lowered. When the mug was empty, he put it down on the wooden kitchen table.

'Is there any more? My throat feels as though I've swallowed half the ocean.'

Silently, I refilled it. 'And your name is?' I prompted.

His blue eyes looked at me over the rim of the mug.

'Now that's a very good question. And if I knew the answer, I'd be only too pleased to tell you.'

'What d'you mean?' I said, frowning at him.

'You must have a name.'

His mouth tilted slightly. 'Oh, I'm sure I have. It's just that I don't know what it is.'

'Don't know?' I echoed.

'No,' he said. 'And before you ask—I don't know where I've come from or even what I was doing in that boat.'

CHAPTER TWO

'You've no idea who are you?' I couldn't believe what the man was saying to me.

'Not the slightest.'

'But surely . . .'

His mouth tightened. 'All I know is I was in that boat when it hit the rocks, and then I was aware of you bending over me. Nothing more. I'm sorry, but that's it.'

'But you must remember something,' I insisted. 'No-one forgets their name.'

'Well, I have.' He pulled the damp towel more closely round his bare shoulders and shivered.

'You need a hot bath,' I said. 'I'll go and run one. Help yourself to more tea, if you want some. Come on, Jamie. Back you go to bed.'

'But, Mummy, what about Matthew?'

'Oh, I'm sure he'll be back with you again by tomorrow.'

When I went back to the kitchen after

settling Jamie and running the bath, the man was hunched down in his chair, head resting on the table, deeply asleep. I stood, looking down at him, wondering what to do.

He was probably in his mid-thirties. Fairly tall, as I'd discovered when I tried to help him up the beach. With his deeply-tanned skin, he obviously spent a lot of time outdoors. It was a tan that had built up over the years, not from a brief holiday. And judging by the long bare leg that my pink bath towel hardly covered, a great deal of him was tanned. Now that his hair had dried, it was not so dark either. Sort of a warm honey-colour. And I knew his eyes were blue.

His wet jeans and sweatshirt were draped over another chair, and I picked them up to put into the washing machine before the sea-water ruined them. The labels were well-known brands, but not expensive.

Turning, I searched for his shoes—and remembered that he hadn't been wearing any.

I wondered whether there other people on that boat and, if so, what had happened to them. In the darkness I hadn't been able to see how big it was. Everything had happened far too quickly.

There were so many questions I needed to ask him when he woke. But if his memory was gone . . .

It was probably just from shock. By the morning, he'd be all right again, I decided, switching on the washing-machine and hearing its gentle hum begin.

At the sound, the man stirred, slightly raising his head, and for a moment I thought he was going to wake, then his breathing deepened and he was still again.

Lightning flickered across the sky, but now it was a long way off and the thunder only a faint murmur. The force of the storm had passed.

Tomorrow it would be forgotten.

I looked down at the sleeping man. And tomorrow he would be gone.

Jamie woke me, as he always did, bouncing on to the end of my bed, eager for us to go down to the beach. It fascinated him and he was quite content to spend hours there, searching the rock pools and wandering the shoreline for treasure.

I struggled from the depths of sleep, reluctant to open my eyes. 'Oh, Jamie,' I murmured. 'It's been such a short night. Why don't you go back to bed and read one of your books for a while?'

'No, Mummy. It's morning-time. Look.'

He stretched up and tugged at the faded flowered curtains, pulling them back from the salt-hazed window. A startlingly bright ray of sunshine dazzled in and I closed my eyes quickly.

'Jamie! Please!' I groaned, burying my face in the pillow.

'The man is making you some tea, Mummy.'

The man!

Panic-stricken, I was out of bed, sliding my arms into the sleeves of my dressing-gown and tying up the belt before I reached the door. My feet hardly touched the stairs as I ran down them, with Jamie at my heels.

I heard the fridge open as I went into the kitchen. The man's head turned.

'You don't mind, do you?' He held up a carton of milk.

I shook my head.

The pink towel was draped round his waist like a skirt, and I noticed a wooden clothes peg held it in place.

He followed the direction of my eyes and his mouth twitched. 'The wretched thing kept falling off and I couldn't find where you'd put my clothes. Would you like tea or coffee?'

Picking up the previous night's mugs, he rinsed them under the tap and put them back on the table. I watched in amazement. He certainly seemed to be making himself at home.

'Orange juice, please,' Jamie said, going to join him. 'It's in that bottle on the shelf. Mummy doesn't let me have too much though, 'cos it's full of sugar.'

'Right then, Jamie, orange juice it is. And what about Mummy?'

'I'll make my own,' I said tersely, spooning coffee into a mug. How dare a total stranger

12

take over like this.

Hearing the annoyance in my tone, his amused expression changed. 'I'm sorry,' he said quietly. 'I just wanted to do something to help. I wouldn't be alive today if you hadn't dragged me out of the sea. Making a cup of coffee is poor return for saving my life.'

I smiled wryly back at him and held out the mug for him to fill.

His voice was different. No longer hoarse from the salt-water he'd swallowed, it was deep and warm. The sort of voice that would have a soothing effect if listened to for any length of time.

Not that I was going to listen to it for any length of time, I hasted to tell myself. Once his clothes were dry, he would be gone. I opened the washing-machine and lifted them out, transferring them to the tumble drier.

'Ah, so that's where they were. If you show me where the bread is, I'll make some toast.'

I felt my shoulders stiffen. He was doing it again. Taking over as though this cottage was his own.

'Oh, dear,' he said, obviously reading my expression.

'No, it's all right. Go ahead. There's a sliced loaf in the larder. I'll do some eggs. Scrambled or fried?'

We sat round the kitchen table like a family should. All three of us. Once, it had been like that when I was married to Tim. How it

13

probably was with his new wife and her children. Did they call him Daddy now, as Jamie did?

A wave of bitterness flooded over me. How could he do such a thing to his own son? Cutting off all communication.

'It's better that way, Becca,' he told me.

Better for whom? Not Jamie. How could anyone be so callous? But then, all men were probably the same.

I sliced savagely into my scrambled egg and was aware of the man's eyes studying me.

'Have you remembered your name?' I asked.

His mouth tightened as he shook his head.

'That's strange,' I said, trying not to show my disbelief.

'Why?'

'Oh, come on! You can't have forgotten everything. After all, you know how to look in someone's fridge for milk and make coffee and tea.'

'And toast,' Jamie chimed in, his eyes growing wide and anxious as he listened to us.

'Probably automatic actions. Deeply instilled into me throughout life,' the man said, and I saw that his eyes were again full of laughter.

'It's not funny,' I snapped.

'I know,' he said. 'And let me assure you, it isn't.'

Instantly, I felt contrite. Here I was, blaming the poor man for losing his memory, without even considering just how terrible it must be for him.

'And I haven't even got any shoes.' His voice sounded solemn, until I saw his mouth was quivering with laughter, and couldn't help myself from joining in.

Jamie stretched out his hand and put it on the man's bare arm. 'You can use my flip-flops. They haven't got any fronts or backs, so they might fit on your feet.'

'Thank you, Jamie,' he said, wiggling his toes. 'That's very kind of you, but somehow . . .'

'D'you think, if we go down to the beach, we could find something washed up from the boat that might give us a clue?' I suggested, putting my knife and fork together and taking the plates over to the sink.

'Treasure!' Jamie shrieked, rushing to the kitchen door. 'Matthew said there be treasure.'

The man frowned and turned to me. 'Who is this Matthew?'

I smiled. 'Jamie's imaginary friend. He suddenly materialised soon after we came to stay here.'

'Stay here? You're on holiday?'

'No,' I said abruptly, turning on the hot tap and swirling the first plate under it. 'Starting a new life. Look, the tumble drier's switched itself off. Your clothes should be ready now to put back on and you won't need shoes on the beach.'

15

CHAPTER THREE

The sea was a deep azure, reflecting the clear blue of the sky, making it difficult to remember how ferocious the storm had been the previous night. Tiny waves quivered along the shoreline where wading birds strutted. Here and there thick strands of seaweed littered the shingle and sand in untidy heaps— and among them lay spars of splintered wood.

Jamie was already racing on ahead, when I saw the man hesitate, the bones of his face taut under his skin as his jaw clenched.

'Would you rather not have come down here with us?'

For a moment he didn't reply and I saw his throat jerk as he swallowed several times. Why, I wondered, is he so reluctant? What does he expect to find? Were there others on the boat with him? Does he really not know?

And then I noticed Jamie. He was standing ankle-deep in the shallow water, his head turned sideways, deep in conversation. Matthew had returned.

I watched my son's head nod; saw him scamper over the shingle to where a tangle of seaweed was bobbing among the rocks. My heart began to pound.

'Jamie! Stop!'

Whether it was the fierceness of my cry, I

don't know, but for once he obeyed instantly and twisted round to look questioningly at me.

'Matthew says there be treasure, Mummy.'

'Stay there,' I ordered, forgetting the man as I ran. Whatever—or whoever—was caught up in that weed, I didn't want it to be found by my little son.

With shaking legs, I moved towards it, my feet sliding on loose shingle, still wet from the receding tide. The seaweed sank and rose in the swell of each wave, draping itself like a shining shawl over the rocks until, finally, it rested on a flat shelf of granite.

Reaching out one hand, I parted the strands, dreading what I might touch. And then I stopped, my back straightening.

What was I thinking? This was all in my son's imagination. There was no Matthew. There was no treasure. And here was I—believing it.

A wave washed gently across the rock, lifting seaweed, retreating again with it held high, leaving a shallow pool.

I glanced down. Something floated on the surface of the water, but before the next wave could seize it, I'd picked it up and was prising apart the sodden pages.

A man's face, blotched and distorted, but still recognisable, stared back at me from the covers of a passport.

'What have you found, Mummy? Is it treasure?' Jamie's voice called. 'Can I come

17

and see?'

With sand flying up around his running feet, he raced towards me, but the man reached me first. The blue of his eyes had turned to steel as he snatched the wet pages from my cold fingers.

'It is you, isn't it?' I said.

'Could be,' he replied, his voice uneven. 'Or someone who looks similar. It's difficult to tell, having been soaked by the sea. And the writing is impossible to read.'

'Not all of it,' I said, smoothing out the page. 'There's a name . . . It looks like a B or possibly a D.'

'Does it?' He sounded unconvinced.

'Let me see, let me see. Please, Mummy. It's my treasure. Matthew told me.'

Jamie peered at the passport the man held out to him. 'Oh,' he said, in disappointment. 'Not treasure at all.'

'Perhaps it is,' I said. 'It might tell us a lot, once we dry it out. Let's go back to the cottage and see.'

'But I want to find real treasure, Mummy. Matthew said there'd be some. Let's go on looking. Please.'

'Just for a little while then.'

'Must we?' The man's voice was weary.

'You're tired after all that ordeal,' I said. 'Go and rest. Jamie and I won't be long.'

I was a little wary about taking Jamie too far along the beach. Splintered bits of wood

18

drifted to and fro on the waves and more were scattered over the rocks as the tide ebbed. I wasn't sure what we might find. It could be another washed-up body.

Had the man been alone on the boat? And where was he going? Where had he been? Was he a fisherman? If so, surely someone would have missed him by now. But perhaps he wasn't local. The thoughts flitted through my mind like butterflies.

Jamie's face puckered with disappointment. 'Matthew told me there was treasure, Mummy. He said it was a treasure ship.'

'Well, there doesn't seem to be any treasure on this beach,' I told him. 'Let's go back now. Maybe when the tide has gone right out, we'll find something.'

His face brightened. 'Yes, Mummy. We'll come back again then.'

As we climbed up the shingle, I could see a car winding down the narrow track towards the cottage. By the time we reached there it was parked outside and I realised it was the police.

An officer was already talking to the man, when I left Jamie outside making sandcastles, while I went into the lounge.

'Should have reported it straight away, Sir,' he was saying. 'Coastguards should've been told. What was the name of your vessel? I'll get on to them now.'

'I'm afraid he's lost his memory,' I explained quickly, butting in. 'He has no idea of who he is, or anything.'

'No memory? Been to the hospital, have you, Sir?'

'It's only ten o'clock, officer.' The man yawned. 'This young lady dragged me out of the sea in the middle of last night's storm. I've slept ever since.' He pointed to a plaid blanket and pillow crumpled on the sofa. 'You can see you've just woken me.'

I stared at him. But that wasn't true. The man's gaze caught and held mine, and I read desperation in his eyes.

'Then I suggest the sooner you see a doctor, the better, Sir.' The policeman closed his notebook. 'Should've been reported straight away though. I'll have to let the coastguard know what's happened, then I'll be back again later to see how you're faring.' He turned to me. 'I'll leave it to you to make sure he gets medical attention, Madam. Good morning to you both.'

I closed the door behind him and swung round to face the man. 'Why didn't you show him the passport?'

He chewed a corner of his lip. 'I'm not sure. It was just a feeling. I need to know more about myself before I do that. I could be some sort of criminal, couldn't I? Drug-runner. Smuggler. Anything.'

'What makes you say that?' I asked, with a smile. 'You could be a fisherman, or just someone who likes sailing.'

The tense lines of his face relaxed as he smiled back at me. 'Of course I could, but I need to prove that first before . . .' He paused. 'I know it's a bit of a liberty, but can I stay on here? Just until I sort myself out? My memory is bound to return in a day or two.'

Clearly he read the doubtful expression on my face. 'No, I'm sorry,' he said quickly. 'That wasn't fair of me. After all, why should you take the risk? I'll find a hotel.'

'And how do you intend to pay?' I enquired drily. 'So far your wallet hasn't been washing up, or a suitable set of credit cards. Not even any shoes. Somehow I doubt a hotel will welcome you.'

CHAPTER FOUR

'If you are going to stay here, we'll have to call you something,' I said. 'What name would you like?'

His forehead wrinkled, then cleared. 'Let Jamie choose.'

'Matthew'll know. I'll go and ask him.'

I watched my son climb up onto the window seat; saw him cup his hand round his mouth as he leaned sideways to whisper into the empty space beside him; heard him chuckle before he came running back to us.

'Matthew says your name be Daniel,' he

said.

A slight shiver went down my spine as I remembered the blurred letters on the passport and one that could have been a B or a D. I looked closely at the man, but his face revealed nothing.

'OK then, Daniel it is—until we discover my real name.'

Jamie curled himself, cat-like, onto the window seat again, gazing out through the hazy glass, his head turning every now and then and nodding, as if in conversation. I saw Daniel watching him with a puzzled expression.

'What happened to the passport?' I said, wanting to divert him.

'It's drying out.'

'Where?'

'The oven. It seemed the warmest place.'

Crossing the kitchen, I tugged open the door and stepped back as a wave of heat rushed out, searing into my face. On one of the shelves the passport lay, brown and crumbling. Holding it by a corner, I pulled it out, dropped it onto the floor, and saw it disintegrate into a scorched heap.

'Oh dear.'

Was there a note of triumph in Daniel's voice, I wondered, or was it genuine regret?

'Don't worry,' he said mildly. 'It probably had nothing to do with me. Anyway, aren't you supposed to take me to see a doctor before that policeman comes back?'

'I don't know a doctor here,' I snapped.

'Try the *Yellow Pages*.'

I glared at him. 'For a man with no memory, you seem to remember an awful lot.'

He shrugged. 'Maybe some things are ingrained. We'll have to ask the doctor, won't we—if and when we find one.'

The phone directory revealed three names. None of them anywhere local.

'Try phoning the surgeries to see which one can fit me in today,' he suggested.

'Why don't you?' I said, tossing the book onto his lap.

'OK, but they'll probably think it's a hoax. Shipwrecked mariner. No memory. It does sound a bit far-fetched, doesn't it?'

'You said it,' I replied dryly, and started to tap out the first number.

The third doctor could give him an emergency appointment at 2.20 pm, the receptionist said, and asked his name. I explained about the lost memory.

'But I must have a name,' she persisted.

'Daniel,' I replied.

'Mr Daniels?' came the question.

'That'll do.'

'You'd better come in to see him with me,' Daniel said, while we sat in the waiting room and he was adjusting the laces of a pair of trainers we'd bought in a charity shop next door to the surgery.

'No way. I can't leave Jamie on his own.'

Daniel stepped over to the receptionist. 'You don't mind keeping an eye on this little boy, while we see the doctor, do you?'

She smiled coyly up at him. 'Of course not, Mr Daniels. I quite understand if your wife would like to go in with you.'

'But I'm not . . .' I began.

'The doctor can see you now.'

She held open the door and ushered us inside.

Once we were in there, Daniel left it to me to explain what had happened. Not that there was much to tell. I pointed out how I'd rescued him from the sea after his boat had been wrecked in the storm, and that he had no idea of who he was or where he'd come from.

'Not surprising,' the doctor observed, as he gave Daniel a swift examination. 'Any headache? Dizziness? Nausea? Doesn't appear to be any physical damage, apart from a few nasty abrasions and some bruising. Shouldn't worry, if I were you. Dare say everything will return in a day or so. If not, come and see me again. Good afternoon.'

We were back in the waiting room within minutes and the next patient was being guided in through his door.

The receptionist looked up as we appeared. 'No trouble at all, your little boy. Drawn a lovely picture of you and your wife on your boat, Mr Daniels. Look.'

She held out a pencilled drawing. It was a rather basic sailing boat, with two figures seated at either end. One had long curly hair.

'Mr Daniels? Are you all right?'

She ran forward from behind her desk, and between us we caught Daniel as he crumpled to the floor.

'Only fainted. Bit weak after that accident. Not surprising,' the doctor commented, bending over him. 'Be all right in a moment or two. Nasty shock, I daresay. Make sure he gets plenty of rest. Feeling better now, old chap?'

Daniel's eyes fluttered open and he lifted his head, gazing blankly round the waiting-room.

'You stay here for a minute or two, old chap. Don't rush. Like a glass of water? That's it then. Sit yourself down on this chair. Be all right in no time. Don't forget, come and see me again if you're still feeling under the weather in a day or so.'

It was another ten minutes before Daniel was ready to be driven back to the cottage. His face was very drawn and even with his tan, he looked pale, and I noticed his hands shaking as he struggled to do up the seat-belt.

But why? What made him collapse like that? The doctor had found nothing physically wrong.

Jamie was very quiet. His eyes worried as he sat on the back seat of the car, still clutching his picture.

His picture. It was when Daniel looked at it that he'd passed out. A drawing of a sailing boat with two figures in it—a man and a woman.

So was there someone else in that boat when it was driven onto the rocks? A woman?

Daniel's wife or girlfriend?

The doctor had said it was only a matter of time before his memory returned. A couple of days, maybe. Then Daniel, or whatever his name was, would be gone.

Yet, somehow, I felt uneasy—sure that Daniel knew more than he was revealing.

But the boat had gone onto the rocks and been wrecked. There was no question about that. And he had almost drowned. There was no question about that either. So why didn't I trust him?

As the car bumped down the rutted track towards the cove, I glanced sideways at him. His eyes were closed and he looked completely exhausted. Like someone emotionally drained. If it was all an act, he was very convincing.

A car was parked on the shingle beside the cottage when I drew up and I could see two dark figures near the rocks.

'Daniel,' I said, rousing him, and pointed.

His head jerked upright and for a moment his eyes were dazed, then I saw his expression sharpen. One hand reached out, opening the door.

'Have they found something?'

26

'I don't know but, look, they're coming back.'

We stood, side by side, watching the two men—one, short and thickset; the other, younger and taller—slowly climb up the shelving beach.

When they reached us, the short one held out an identification card showing he was a Detective Inspector, and I wondered why someone like that should be interested in a wrecked boat.

'Find anything?' I asked.

'Not yet,' he replied, scratching the corner of his mouth with a nicotine-stained finger. 'Sending divers down later. Must be quite a bit of the boat still on the sea-bed. Not much been cast ashore. Need to get the name.'

He looked questioningly at Daniel. 'That missing memory of yours returned yet, Sir?'

Daniel shook his head. 'We've just been to the doctor. He says it could take months—and possibly not at all.'

Surprised, I opened my mouth to correct him. That wasn't what the doctor had said. But before I could speak, I felt Daniel's fingers grip my wrist, and when I turned to looked at him, his blue eyes were full of warning.

CHAPTER FIVE

Seeing the expression on Daniel's face, I didn't say a word. But why was he looking at me like that? Why wasn't he telling the truth yet again? Slowly, I felt his fingers relax round my wrist.

'Salvage boat should be here any time now,' the Inspector said, his gaze fixed on Daniel. 'And once they've carried out their investigation, we'll soon have the answers to everything. That'll be a great relief to you, won't it, Sir?'

From his tone, I guessed he didn't believe Daniel either. 'I suggest you take the little lad and go inland for the rest of the day. There's going to be a lot happening round here. Don't want him getting upset, do you?'

He gave me a meaningful nod and smiled down at Jamie, who stood hand in mine.

'You go, Becca,' Daniel said quickly. 'I'll stay here and get some rest. I'm shattered.'

'It would be best if you went with them, Sir. You won't get much rest here, with all the commotion that'll be going on.'

A flurry of thin rain swept across the cove, misting it like gauze. I shivered at the sudden coldness. 'We'll all stay,' I said, pulling the key out of my jeans pocket and moving towards the door. 'There's no point in trailing round

28

somewhere, getting soaked.'

'Not a good idea, Ma'am. Better if you do as I suggest.'

'We'll stay,' I repeated firmly, bundling Jamie inside and holding the door open as Daniel followed, then slamming it shut behind him.

'Was that a wise thing to do?' he asked, sinking into an armchair and resting his head against the back of it.

I shrugged. 'I prefer to make my own decisions.'

His mouth curved. 'So I've noticed. Shall I put the kettle on, or will you?'

'There's a 'normous boat coming,' Jamie shrieked from the window-seat. 'Quick, Mummy! Come and see.'

Daniel and I joined him, leaning forward to peer through the rain-spattered glass.

The salvage vessel had arrived. Several vehicles were already coming down the track, crunching on to the shingle, doors banging as men jumped out, shouting to each other. The rain intensified, rattling against the windows and the sky darkened.

'Have you made a decision?'

I stared blankly at Daniel. 'Decision?'

Laughter twitched the corners of his lips. 'About the kettle.'

'How can you joke when . . .' I waved a hand towards the window. '. . . all that's going on out there?'

'At least it's better than watching and waiting.'

'What do you think they're going to find then?'

'The answer to everything—isn't that what that Inspector said? I suppose, once they discover the name of the boat, things will move forward. If I own it, then they'll find out exactly who I am.'

'And if you don't own it?' I asked, turning on the tap and holding the kettle under it.

'Someone does,' he said quietly. 'Maybe that person will know.'

'Mummy! Come and see. There's people with feet like frogs and funny things on their faces. Look, they're jumping into the sea. Now they've disappeared. Are they looking for the treasure?'

'Jamie, why don't you come in the kitchen?' I suggested. 'It's nearly tea-time. How about grating cheese for the sauce, while I cook some pasta? You like doing that, don't you?'

'Not today, Mummy. Matthew and I want to watch the diving men. There's a helicopter zooming over the cliffs now. It's really, really 'citing.'

'Jamie!'

'Ooh, the boat has rope-bits coming out of it. They're going right down into the waves with the diver-men. Mummy! Mummy! Matthew says they've found the treasure.'

Another flurry of rain lashed against the

window, coursing down the glass in thin rivers, then eased a little. As it cleared, I saw the shattered boat, water cascading from it, by the side of the salvage boat. Black heads bobbed in the water, fixing lines that snaked back to a winch on one of the vehicles.

Daniel stood as if carved from wood, the profile of his face sharply defined like a silhouette.

I stood beside him, my hands resting on Jamie's shoulders, watching the scene outside as though it were a film in slow-motion.

An engine roared and I saw the cables go taut as the remains of the boat gradually reached the shore and were hauled on to a long trailer.

Slowly, the vehicles lining the beach reversed, sending tiny stones flying out from under their wheels. Headlights blazed, lighting up the room as they swung round, and I saw Daniel's whole body slump like an empty glove puppet.

'So now we wait,' I said, watching the helicopter vanish over the cliffs.

'Yes,' he agreed. 'Now we wait.'

'Well, it's no good just sitting here. Come on, Jamie. We'll go and make that pasta.'

I was tipping spaghetti into a saucepan of boiling water, when someone rapped on the front door. Surely the police couldn't be back already?

When I opened it, a girl stood, outlined in

the doorway, clothes drenched from the rain. With one wet hand she held out a damp card.

'Please,' she said, pushing a tangle of dripping hair away from her face. 'Just five minutes. I saw the salvage boat and helicopter and everything, and thought you might know what it was all about.'

I held the door wider. 'You'd better come in.'

'Who is it?' Daniel called from the lounge.

'A reporter—from the local newspaper. You never know, a bit of publicity might help find out who you are, Daniel.'

I saw the girl's face brighten.

Fifteen minutes later we'd told her the whole story.

'That's really fantastic,' she said, slipping the tiny tape-recorder back into her bag. 'I've only been in this job a month and this is my first real scoop. D'you mind if I use my mobile to let my editor know? Then he can leave space in tomorrow's edition.'

Holding the phone, she stood up and moved round the room as she spoke.

'Mummy!' Jamie's plaintive voice came from the kitchen. 'Can I stop grating cheese now? It's filled the whole bowl.'

'I'm so sorry. I didn't realise you were about to have your meal,' the girl said, picking up her cagoule, and headed swiftly for the door. 'Bye.'

I quite thought the police would return, or at least phone, with some kind of news later

32

that evening, but they didn't. Daniel ate hardly any of his pasta, abruptly pushing the plate away and leaving the table. Seconds later, I heard the door slam and, through the window, saw him heading for the beach.

There was nothing I could do. I couldn't follow him. He wasn't a prisoner. But I still felt anxious. In the dusk, I could see him striding along the tide-line, towards the rocks. When he reached them, he stood, staring out across the waves, the wind twisting his rain-wet hair.

Will the wreck of that boat reveal the answer to all his questions? I wondered. And if it does, what then? His whole life must be hidden away, somewhere, like a locked box.

It was quite dark when he returned. Jamie was already tucked up in bed, asleep, and I was reading—or trying to read—a book, but the words had no meaning. My whole mind was filled with Daniel and the torment he must be suffering.

I heard the back door open, then close; the clink of a glass and water run from the tap, before he came into the room where I was sitting. His face and clothes were wet, and he stood, looking down at me, his eyes filled with desolation.

'Any news, Becca?'

I shook my head.

His mouth tightened. 'I need to know what they've discovered. They must have found out something by now. Why don't they tell me?'

33

'Perhaps there wasn't enough of the boat left?' I suggested.

'Oh, for goodness' sake! You saw it. Part of it was holed by the rocks, yes, but there was plenty there to identify.'

'Maybe not its name though.'

He paced up and down the room like a caged animal, the contours of his face taut, and his voice was harsh as he said, 'But I have to know.'

A huge wave was racing towards the beach, so high that I couldn't see the top of it, and Daniel was standing by the rocks, directly in its path. My body was rigid, every limb frozen, unable to move, no matter how I tried.

I opened my mouth to shout at him. Tell him to run. But no words came. And the wave grew, rising higher and higher, until it blotted out the whole sky. Then it began to descend . . .

I was still trying to call Daniel's name, when I woke to see him bending over me. Stubble darkened his chin and his eyes were red-rimmed from lack of sleep, but his mouth was smiling.

'Bad dreams?' he asked, holding out a mug of tea.

I nodded, rubbing a wary hand over my stiff neck as I raised my head from the back of the chair, realising I must have fallen asleep while I sat there the night before.

'You were making strange noises, so I

thought I'd better wake you. Sorry about that. It's still very early. Drink this. It'll make you feel better.'

With shaking fingers, I took the mug he offered, slowly sipping the welcome liquid, and the dream began to slip away.

'Did you sleep?' I questioned.

He wrinkled his nose. 'Not really. But you did.' He gave me a quizzical look. 'Did you know you snore?'

'I don't!'

'Oh, yes you do! Very delicately, I must say, but snoring it was.'

He moved over to the window and pulled back the curtain. Outside, it was almost impossible to decide where the sea ended and the sky began, but even as I watched, a slight line of gold appeared, defining the horizon. Slowly, it changed colour, first pink, then darker red, until within minutes a slight arc of scarlet appeared, growing larger and brighter like a ball of fire, before it rose from the sea in a blaze of dazzling colour.

Somehow, with the dawn, Daniel seemed more relaxed. Maybe he had slept after all. Tiredness can be soul-destroying.

We were still eating breakfast when the crunch of tyres on stones came down the track. I glanced out of the window. The Inspector was back. Daniel had opened the door even before the car stopped.

'Good morning.' The man coughed throatily

as he came into the kitchen. 'Sorry to interrupt your meal, but I was sure you'd want to know the result of our investigation first-hand. It's not quite the same over the phone, is it? Do I smell coffee? I wouldn't say no to a cup.'

It was as if he enjoyed taking his time, delaying what he had to say. Silently, he waited while I rinsed a mug and filled it, before passing him the milk jug and sugar bowl.

Daniel chewed his lower lip and I could sense his frustration, while the Inspector stirred in sugar and began to drink, his slightly bloodshot eyes watching us over the top of the mug.

'Very nice,' he murmured, brushing the back of his hand across his mouth. 'Now, shall we sit down.'

I perched myself on the edge of the table, but Daniel remained standing and I saw his hand clench, his knuckles white.

'Well now, Sir, we've established the vessel is, or should I say was, *The Lady Jane*. Does that ring any bells with you?'

Daniel shook his head, but I thought his eyes narrowed slightly.

'Has a mooring over at Falmouth . . .' The Inspector paused and rubbed the side of his nose.

'So you have a name for the owner?' Daniel's voice was sharp.

'Oh yes, Sir, we have a name for the owner. Trevose. Daniel Trevose.' Coffee spilled from

36

my mug on to the floor. Was it sheer chance that Jamie's imaginary friend Matthew had said he was called Daniel?

'So Mr Trevose, there are a few more matters we'd like to discuss with you at the station.'

'What matters?' Daniel demanded.

'Oh, let's wait until we get there, shall we?'

'I'd prefer to be told now.'

'Well, Sir, there were items discovered on board.'

'What items?'

'Do we have to go into all that now, Sir—in front of the lady?'

'I asked what items.'

The Inspector drained his mug and put it carefully down on the table. 'Narcotic substances. Various types. I dare say you'll be fully aware of what I'm talking about.'

Daniel's tone was cold. 'No, I'm not. If you remember, I've lost my memory.'

'So you say, Sir. Anyway, we can discuss all that when we get to the station.'

'I'm not going anywhere until you can prove who I am. The boat may be owned by this Daniel Trevose, but why should it be me?'

The Inspector frowned and his voice was hard when he spoke again. 'You were on it, Sir. What other proof do we need?'

Daniel gave a cynical laugh. 'A great deal more, I should say. Just because I was on the boat, doesn't mean I own it.'

'No,' he agreed. 'But you were on a vessel carrying narcotic substances and until evidence can be produced to show that these didn't belong to you, then further questioning is necessary.'

He stood up and began to button his jacket. 'Do you wish me to formally charge you, Sir, or will you accompany me voluntarily?'

Daniel turned to look at me, his mouth a thin tight line. 'I'm sorry, Becca.' Then, tugging his sweatshirt over his head, he led the way out through the door.

'Why's that man taken Daniel away?' Jamie asked, frowning up at me, as he chewed cornflakes.

I collected plates and bowls and took them over to the sink. 'He wants to ask Daniel some questions.'

'Why?'

'He thinks the boat belongs to Daniel.'

'It does belong to Daniel. And there be treasure on board. Matthew says so.'

He twisted round to look across the room, and my spine iced as I watched his face, eyebrows raised in questions, then saw him nod. 'It be valuable treasure, Matthew says.'

Valuable treasure—which is what narcotics are to those who deal in them. I couldn't believe Daniel was a drug smuggler. He didn't seem like a criminal. But then how do you tell?

With such a precious cargo, he wouldn't want to be too far from the wreck of his boat, would he? No wonder he spent so much time on the beach. He was searching to find what was washed up.

I turned on the tap and plunged the dishes into the sink, angrily scrubbing them clean. He'd certainly conned me into believing him.

Jamie curled himself up at one end of the window-seat, nose pressed to the glass. I swilled away the dirty water and went to join him.

'Careful, Mummy! Don't sit on Matthew.'

I stepped back, warily viewing the space next to my son. An imaginary friend was all very well, but this one was taking up too much of my son's life for my liking.

'Let's go for a walk, sweetheart.'

If I stayed indoors, I'd only be thinking about Daniel, wondering what was happening. They'd probably formally arrested him by now.

It always surprised me just how quickly the weather could change in Cornwall. One day, ferocious gales and torrential rain; the next, clear blue skies and endless sunshine. Today was like that.

Jamie ran on ahead, stopping every now and then to pick up tiny shells or gleaming stones, and bring them back in sandy hands to show me. We were both admiring a jewel-like scrap of green glass, polished smooth by the sea, when I heard the scrunch of shingle, and looked up.

A man was walking towards me, silhouetted

39

against the sun, so that I was dazzled by it.

'Daniel!' I cried out, surprised that the police had released him so quickly. But as he came closer, I noticed he was wearing different clothes—a pale suede jacket, navy trousers and blue check shirt—not the worn denims and faded sweatshirt I'd last seen him in.

And then I realised it wasn't Daniel at all, but someone who could have been his double.

CHAPTER SIX

As the man came closer, his resemblance to Daniel was even greater. The only difference was his immaculate appearance and absence of the wounds that scarred Daniel after his battle with the sea and rocks.

He smiled, and it was as though Daniel was smiling at me—the same crinkling of his eyes and upward curve of his lips.

'You must be Rebecca Bassett,' he said, and I wondered how he knew my name.

'There's been a lot about you in the newspaper,' he explained, reading my puzzled expression. 'How you rescued my brother, Daniel.'

'Your brother?'

'Yes, I'm Barry Trevose.'

His fingers closed round mine with a firm grip. 'I came to thank you, and to take him home. Is he indoors?'

'No,' I said slowly, not sure how to go on. How do you tell someone that their brother has been arrested?

His expression changed and I saw that his eyes were quite different from Daniel's. Much paler, hardly blue at all.

'Where is he then? I thought he was staying here with you.'

'The policeman's taken him away.'

I'd forgotten Jamie was standing beside me, listening intently.

'Police?' Barry Trevose's voice sharpened.

'They found narcotics hidden on the boat,' I explained.

'You mean Daniel's been arrested?'

I nodded.

'What about the boat? Where have they taken that?'

'I don't know. After the divers found it yesterday, it was winched up and hauled off somewhere. The police came early this morning—and took Daniel away for questioning.'

'What did he tell them?'

'I've no idea. Not much I should imagine.' I frowned at him. 'You do realise your brother has lost his memory, don't you? He was badly knocked about when the boat was wrecked on those rocks over there and . . .'

Before I could finish, Barry Trevose interrupted me. 'Yes, yes, I read all that in the

41

newspaper, but no-one can possibly forget everything.'

'Well, Daniel has,' I replied abruptly.

'And you believe him?'

I hesitated.

'You don't.' Barry Trevose gave a short laugh. 'And you're quite right, too. My brother can put on a very convincing act when he wants to. He's a good con-man, although I doubt he'll fool the police for long.'

'The doctor did say . . .'

'Amnesia? Caused by all that trauma? Oh, I'm sure Daniel gave a very plausible performance. It's not difficult, is it? So where have they taken him? I'd better go and try to bail him out.'

'To the nearest police station, I suppose, but I've no idea where that is. Do you live in this area? You said you'd read about it in the local paper.'

'Oh, better than that! It was in all the tabloids this morning. Mystery man washed up on Cornish beach or words to that effect, depending on which paper it was in. When I recognised Daniel's photograph, I came here straight away.'

That young reporter hasn't wasted much time, I thought. But how . . . And then I remembered—mobile phones send photos, so it would have been easy for her. No wonder she was moving round the room while she spoke to her editor. Probably making sure she had several suitable photos of Daniel to pass on.

At least it had done some good. His brother would never have known otherwise. Now I didn't have to bother any more. Barry Trevose would take all responsibility for Daniel.

And yet the idea didn't make me feel happy. Even in such a short time, I'd grown used to having Daniel here. I liked his humour. I liked him.

But should I? His brother painted a very different picture of him. A con-man. That's what he said. Putting on a convincing act.

I knew only too well that Daniel hadn't been truthful with the police. That passport. Telling them that the doctor said his memory may never return. Why?

Narcotics had been found on his boat. There was no disputing that. So Daniel must have known they were there. And if he did, then it was quite obvious what he was doing— smuggling them into the country.

The Cornish coast is riddled with tiny coves and inlets. A small boat could use any of them without being discovered. Smugglers weren't something that only happened in ancient days.

'Tell me more about your brother,' I said. 'Where does he live? What's his job?'

'Some other time. I need to locate this police station and find out what's happening.' Barry Trevose's voice had a hard edge to it and I guessed he was concerned about his brother.

'Thanks for your help. I'll deal with Daniel now.'

'You will let me know . . .' I started to say, but he was already striding across the beach and climbing the shingle bank to where the track began.

Well, that's over, I thought. Jamie and I can settle back into our quiet life again. I glanced across to where my son was wandering along the sand, gathering bits of this and that in his red plastic bucket. For once he didn't appear to be in conversation with Matthew.

I was determined to put Daniel Trevose out of my mind. He wasn't my concern any more. I could forget about him.

So why did I listen to every news bulletin on local radio that day, waiting to hear his name?

All I'd done was rescue the man from the sea. That was now in the past. Life goes on. The new life that Jamie and I must make. My husband, Tim, belonged to someone else, with a different family to care for—and love. Jamie and I were on our own.

After the storm and days of damp, drifting mizzle, the weather changed abruptly. Suddenly it was hot. Clear blue skies turned the sea to deep azure, scarcely ruffled by waves, so that it looked like shimmering silk.

Jamie and I needed summer clothes, so a day later we drove into the nearest town to tour the charity shops and see what bargains I could find. Money was something I had to

44

be careful about, with only occasional maintenance from Tim, and now that he'd moved to New Zealand, that wasn't proving easy.

I'd parked in a multi-storey and we were walking from it, along a narrow alley between some shops, when Jamie let out a shriek.

'Look, Mummy! There's Daniel!' And tugging his hand from mine, he began to run, leaving me to push through the crush of people coming towards me.

'Jamie! Wait!'

But he'd already reached the tall figure and thrown his arms round the man's knees, making him stagger.

'What the blazes . . .'

'Daniel!' I said breathlessly, but the blue eyes that looked back at me were hostile.

Gripping Jamie's arm and yanking him out of the way, he growled, 'Can't you keep that child under control?' and continued walking.

'Daniel?' I said again, but he was already disappearing into the crowd of shoppers.

Jamie's eyes brimmed with tears as he rubbed his shoulder and looked up at me. Quickly I bent to hug him.

Surely Daniel wouldn't behave like that? Or would he? Perhaps his memory had returned and he'd forgotten everything since. Does that happen with amnesia?

He must remember Jamie and me, though. But maybe he didn't want to have anything to

45

do with us any more.

Or could it be his brother, Barry? He'd only seen us for a few minutes when he came to the cottage, looking for Daniel. He wouldn't remember us at all.

I craned my neck, trying to see which direction the man had taken. If it was Barry Trevose, then he'd know what had happened to Daniel. After all, he had gone to the police station to find out.

But it was no use. Whoever he was, he'd completely vanished. There was no reason why I shouldn't go there and find out for myself though—if I really wanted to know.

Only I didn't want to know, did I?

'I'm hungry, Mummy.' Jamie tugged at my hand as we left the second charity shop, carrying a couple of carrier bags filled with an assortment of clothes for us both.

'So am I, darling. Look, there's a shop over there selling filled rolls and pasties. Shall we buy some and eat them in a park?'

It was when I was putting the empty packets into a litterbin that I noticed an ornate signpost. It had arms pointing to various amenities—Library, Toilets, Theatre. One arm read *Police Station*.

For a moment I hesitated. Only for a moment though.

'Come on, Jamie.'

Once inside the building, I began to have doubts. Did I really want to know what had happened to a man like that? A man who smuggled drugs?

'Can I help you, madam?'

It was too late to walk out. 'Well . . . yes. I hope so. It's about Daniel Trevose. I'm the person who rescued him from the sea the other night . . . in the storm . . . when his boat was wrecked. I think he may have been brought here yesterday . . . and I was just wondering . . .'

'Daniel Trevose, you say?' Fingers tapped the keyboard of a computer.

'His brother—Barry Trevose—has he been to see him?'

She studied the screen. 'Barry Trevose did you say? No, he hasn't been here.'

'But he told me that's what he was going to do,' I insisted.

'Well, I'm afraid he hasn't. Apart from a doctor and the duty solicitor, no one has been to see Daniel Trevose. Let me see now. He appeared in court this morning and the case has been deferred for another month.'

'He's still in custody then,' I said.

'Oh, no. Mr Trevose was released.'

'Do you know where he's gone?'

The address she gave stunned me. It was my cottage.

Hardly able to believe what she said, I swung away from the desk, and clutching Jamie's hand, almost ran out of the door.

'Can I have my ice cream now, Mummy?'

I hardly heard my son's plea as I hurried him back to the multi-storey car-park, my thoughts whirling like windmills in my brain.

'Please, Mummy. I was a good boy in the police station, wasn't I, and you said you'd buy me one afterwards, if I was.'

'We'll stop on the way home.'

Piling the bags of clothes into the boot and strapping Jamie into his seat, I started the engine and raced down the steep slopes, slamming on the brakes as a car reversed out of a space in front of me just as we reached the ground floor. The engine stalled; the car behind me hooted its horn while I tried desperately to restart.

Eventually we reached the barrier and I leaned out, sliding my ticket into the machine, seeing the arm slowly rise, and then we were through and out into the road.

We stopped once, at a small store that sold ice cream, and Jamie continued the journey contentedly sucking a striped lolly.

While the car bumped down the rutted track to the beach, my eyes were searching for any sign of Daniel. Would the police have brought him back in the same way as they took him away? Or would he have to find his own way? He had no money.

Sunshine glinted on the sea and heat quivered the air along the sandy shoreline. Gulls hung, almost motionless, in the sky and, apart from the faint drag of shingle as tiny waves receded, everywhere was quiet.

And then I saw him, sitting on a high rock, his arms wrapped round his knees, his head slumped forward. 'Daniel!'

Jamie had unclipped his seatbelt, opened the car door and was scampering over the stones. I saw Daniel's head lift, and then his smile, before he jumped down, catching my son up into his arms, swinging him round and round, while they both laughed.

And my breath caught in my throat. Surely this man couldn't be a criminal?

'Why were you so cross with me in that street?' I heard Jamie ask as I reached them.

Daniel's forehead creased and his eyes were puzzled when he looked towards me. 'Cross with you, Jamie? When?'

'Before I had my pasty in that park. You hurt my arm.' Jamie pulled the neck of his T-shirt sideways and twisted his head. 'Look. It's all red.'

'We thought it was you in the town, but it must have been your brother, Barry,' I said slowly.

'Barry?'

Daniel's body was tense as he lowered Jamie down on to the beach, then straightened up, his eyes questioning me.

'Barry came here—after you were arrested. He'd seen a photo of you in the newspaper. You remember that reporter . . . She sold the story of your shipwreck and loss of memory to

49

the national press.'

'Barry was here?' Daniel's voice was barely a whisper, and then it sharpened. 'He didn't threaten you, did he?'

'Threaten me? No,' I said, mystified by his reaction. 'Why would he do that?'

'I know what he's capable of—and as for hurting Jamie, that's the sort of thing Barry would do, too.'

Suddenly, Barry Trevose's words slid into my mind, 'My brother can put on a very convincing act when he wants to. He's a good con-man . . .'

So which of them was I to believe? One of them had been rough with Jamie in Truro. But was it Daniel, or Barry?'

Seeing Daniel with Jamie now, I couldn't believe he would treat my son in such a rough way. But if this was all an act . . .

'Do you mind me coming back here, Becca?'

How am I to answer that? I wondered.

'I need to stay somewhere until my next court appearance and I don't know anywhere else.'

'Your memory hasn't returned?' I said.

He shook his head. 'The police seemed quite happy about me being here. I tried to phone and ask you, but there was no reply. You were in town.'

'How did you know that?' I snapped.

'You've just told me, Becca.' Raising one

eyebrow, he smiled. 'I think you need a cup of tea. Come on, I'll make some. It's the least I can do.'

Putting out a hand, he touched my bare arm—and I flinched. 'Becca, what's wrong?' His blue yes narrowed slightly. 'It's my brother, isn't it? What's he telling you about me? You can't believe a word he says. Truth and honesty are completely alien to him.'

'For a man with no memory, you seem to know a great deal about your brother,' I commented.

He sighed. 'I've told you before, Becca, some things are deeply embedded in my mind while recent events are hidden.'

'How convenient.'

'Becca, believe me. Please. You know I wouldn't do anything to hurt you or Jamie.'

'My brother can put on a very convincing act when he wants to. He's a good con-man . . .'

Those words of Barry Trevose hung over me.

'Becca?'

Jamie ran across the wet stones and caught hold of Daniel's hand with sandy fingers. 'Matthew says it be tea-time and you're going to make it for Mummy and me.'

Matthew says, I thought, and Matthew is never wrong.

CHAPTER SEVEN

You should start trying to rediscover your memory,' I said, picking up our empty mugs and carrying them to the sink.

'And how do you suggest we do that?'

I noticed Daniel said 'we'.

'Visit places. If your boat was berthed in Falmouth, you could live somewhere close by. How about going over there tomorrow? It might trigger off something.'

'We could,' he said, but didn't look convinced.

'What happened in court this morning?' I asked, rinsing a mug under the hot tap and tipping it upside down on the draining board.

'Not much. I had to give my name—which I pointed out was only what I'd been told—and my address—which I don't know.'

He grinned. 'I'm probably recorded as "of no fixed abode" now, along with all the downs-and-outs who came up after me.'

His expression became serious as he went on. 'The solicitor they'd given me gave details of how I'd been brought out of the sea, after the boat was wrecked, and that I now had amnesia. The police doctor was produced—he'd checked me over yesterday, soon after I was arrested—to confirm my state of health. Then the case was adjourned to await further

52

evidence and my improved health. I had to give an address where I would be staying—so I gave yours. It's the only one I know.'

He gave me a rueful glance. 'I'm sorry. You probably thought you'd seen the last of me and here I am, turned up again like a bad penny. Look, if you want me to go, I'll find somewhere.'

'Where?'

I saw his mouth curve. 'Well, now the weather's warmer, there's always the beach. After all, I am of no fixed abode. Or maybe there's a nice bench somewhere.'

'Daniel! It's not a laughing matter.'

'I know, but I do realise I'm being unfair to you. Just because you rescued me, I don't have to be like that other Old Man of the Sea, who sat on Sinbad's shoulders and refused to let go.'

'Another bit of embedded memory?' I asked dryly.

'I surprise myself sometimes,' he replied. 'Now why should something from the Arabian Nights suddenly come out?'

'Perhaps you're a teacher.'

He wrinkled his nose. 'Do I seem like a teacher?'

'You could be anything.'

'But all you can be sure of is that I'm a criminal.'

'That's not certain,' I said quickly.

'You're very trusting.'

'I have known you for a few days now.'

'And I haven't battered you over the head yet. Is that what you mean?'

'Don't joke, Daniel.'

'What else can I do? I don't know who I am, or what I am. I could be anything. Villain. Vicar. Married. Divorced. Have half a dozen children. I don't know, Becca—and it's driving me mad.'

I put my hand on his clenched fist. 'We will find out, Daniel.'

His fingers uncurled, turning over to close round mine. 'Will we, Becca?' he said, and his voice was filled with torment.

I woke to hear voices the following morning and, looking out of my bedroom window, saw Jamie and Daniel standing bare-foot on the sand, with tiny waves rippling round their ankles. Daniel was patiently showing the child how to skim a stone across the surface of the water, making it bounce.

Slipping quickly into my clothes, I went out into the sunshine to join them.

'Mummy!' Jamie came running towards me. 'Daniel can make his stone jump five times, but mine only goes splash. You try.'

I didn't do any better, but it was good to see Daniel looking more relaxed as he swung back his arm and watched a stone fly across the flat water.

'Falmouth today?' I suggested.

His smile eased away the deep lines around

his mouth. 'OK, Falmouth it is,' he agreed.

It was still early when we reached the edge of the town and parked not far from the Maritime Museum, then walked along Arwenack Street, past tiny shops where narrow passageways gave glimpses of the sea, until we reached Prince of Wales pier.

From the end of the stone jetty, the view stretched away into the distance, with the cranes of the docks raised high over large ships on one side.

Tourists, loaded with bags and cameras, or bent under the weight of bulging rucksacks, were moving cautiously down steep stone steps still wet from the tide to climb aboard the St Mawes ferry, filling its wooden seats on deck, or disappearing inside to peer out through misted windows.

'Can we go on that boat, Mummy?'

'No, darling.'

'Why can't we?'

How could I say—because it costs money? Jamie was too young to understand.

'Another day, maybe,' and caught the sudden look of understanding that Daniel gave me.

'I didn't think,' he groaned, leaning against my shoulder. 'Having me around, not paying my way . . . I must have a bank account somewhere, mustn't I? That was a very expensive boat, so I'm obviously not short of a penny.'

'If the boat was yours.'

'Oh, Becca—how on earth am I going to find out anything? It's like banging my head against the proverbial brick wall. Where do I start?'

'The police found out that *The Lady Jane* was berthed here, and from that they traced your name as owner. Daniel, are you all right?'

His eyes were closed and I saw his knuckles whiten as his hands clenched against his sides, and his teeth bite over his lower lip.

'Jane.' The word whispered out.

'Your boat,' I said. *'The Lady Jane.'*

He sank back on to a seat as if his legs had given way, his head shaking. 'No, Jane—my wife. That's who the boat was named after.'

'Your wife?' I echoed. 'Then she must be worried as to what's . . .'

He shook his head again. 'No, she's dead.'

I stared at him, horror creeping into me. 'Dead? You mean, she was on the boat with you . . .'

His eyes opened slowly and I read the pain in them. 'Jane died . . . a couple of years ago . . . Australia . . . she was visiting her sister . . . a car crash . . . together . . . Jane was twenty-two.'

'Daniel, I'm so sorry.'

'We kept the boat moored here . . . *The Lady Jane* . . . Her father gave it to her . . . A twenty-first birthday present.'

A huge gull flew down from the railings and

56

began to peck at a scrap of bread roll on the ground, joined swiftly by two more, fighting to claim it.

Daniel raised his head, his eyelids clenched tight in concentration. 'I'm trying to recall his name.'

I put my hand on his. 'Don't worry. You've remembered so much already.'

'Not enough,' he said, and his voice was desperate.

With a roar of its engine, the ferry started to back away from the stone pier, slowly turning then, leaving behind a faint smell of fumes, headed out towards the open sea.

'We can go on it one day, can't we, Mummy?' Jamie sighed, corning back to join us from where he'd been watching.

'One day, sweetheart,' I replied, putting my arm round him and giving him a hug.

'Is it elevenses time yet? Matthew and me's very hungry.'

'Coffee, Daniel?' I suggested gently.

He walked along the cobbled street, as though in a daze, letting me guide him, then stopped suddenly outside a bow-fronted shop window and climbed the steps.

'This is where we always had coffee,' he said, holding the door open for us to go inside.

There was a table free at the far end, under a tiny window, overlooking the sea and, having lifted Jamie on to the cushioned bench, he sat down beside him.

'Morning, Mr Trevose. Been reading 'bout you in the papers. Pity about your boat. Nasty old accident that was. Lucky to be alive though, aren't you? Two coffees? And what about the little boy? Orange juice for you, m'dear? And some nice biscuits?'

I looked in surprise at the woman taking our order. She seemed to know Daniel extremely well. He stared back at her and I could see from his expression that he was struggling to remember.

'Anna?'

Her plump cheeks crumpled into dimples. 'Hannah. Now then. Fairly strong, with no sugar. Milk, not cream. That's how you like it, isn't it, Mr Trevose? And you, madam?'

'That'll be fine for me, too,' I said, as she held the coffee jug over my cup.

Daniel touched her arm. 'Hannah, I'm sorry to ask this, but can you tell me where I live?'

A chuckle of laughter bubbled out as she put a glass of orange and plate of home-made currant biscuits in front of Jamie.

'That memory of yours still missing, is it? Said that in the paper. Well now, you and your poor dear wife always stayed with her father over near Feock. Big house, he's got there.'

'And his name is?'

'Oh, Mr Trevose, you're having me on! Why 'tis Peter Carrick, of course. Now you drink that coffee before it gets cold.'

So why, I wondered, didn't Peter Carrick

claim his son-in-law when he read about him in the newspaper?

'Shall we go there?' I asked, watching Daniel's spoon stir round and round in his cup.

'Do you mind?'

'It's what we're here for. Jamie, use your serviette, darling.'

There was a map of Cornwall in the glove compartment of my car, and when we got back to it, I fished it out, to search for Feock, guessing it couldn't be too far away if Daniel and his wife were so well-known in the Falmouth coffee house.

It wasn't and soon we were turning down a tree-lined lane, that twisted narrowly.

'Turn right there,' Daniel said, suddenly pointing to an even narrower lane where a signpost indicated Loe Beach. 'Then it's left about a mile or so further on.'

And as we reached a sharp bend—'Here.'

The steep little hill was hardly wide enough for one car and I hoped we met nothing coming the other way, as we came to the next bend.

'Stop!'

Startled, I slammed on the brake, producing a yell from Jamie in the back seat as he jerked sideways and bumped his head against the window.

'This is it.' A rusting wrought iron gate in a thick laurel hedge.

'I can't park here. Nothing can get past,' I

protested.

'There's some waste ground a little further on. You can use that.' Cautiously, I inched forward round the bend and saw a patch of grassy mud, just about large enough to hold one car, and swung on to it.

'We can't barge in without any warning, can we?' I said, as we all climbed out and began to walk back up the lane.

'He is my father-in-law.'

I shrugged. 'OK then. If you say so.'

The gate was stiff to push, creaking as it opened, and a worn brick path led up three steps, before widening to a patio where several terracotta pots of wilted tulips were lined along it. Lawns, badly in need of cutting, disappeared round the side of the house.

'It looks a bit neglected,' I said. 'D'you think anyone's at home?'

'There's only one way to find out.'

'Can I ring the bell?' Jamie asked, standing on tip-toe to reach.

It buzzed weakly, and he tried again, pressing it with one hand held over the other.

We waited. 'Let's try round the back. Maybe he's in the garden.'

It was deserted. 'Obviously, he's out. Or away.'

Or saw us coming and doesn't want to know, I thought, as we trudged back down the brick path, out through the gate and back to the car.

'Can we go home now, Mummy? Matthew'll be lonely all by himself. And I'm hungry.'

'What d'you think, Daniel? Shall we wait to see if he comes back soon?'

'No, let's go home. We could hang around for ages. I'm sure Peter is the best person to fill in some of the details, and until we find him, we won't get very far.'

The tide was well out when we reached the cove, and I saw that a few more bits of the boat had been washed up among strands of seaweed scattering the shore. Jamie was already tugging at his seat-belt, eager to be out of the car and playing on the beach again.

Running ahead of us, he suddenly stopped and I saw his back straighten. Then I noticed the front door of the cottage was slightly open.

Daniel caught my arm, pulling me backwards as I went to go inside. 'Wait!'

He gave the door a sharp push. I watched it slowly move and Daniel step into the hallway, then bend to pick up something from the floor. Unfolding the sheet of paper, he read it, then silently handed it to me.

Just a few words, scribbled in black.

YOU LOST THE GOODS. NOW YOU OWE ME.

CHAPTER EIGHT

With the note held in my hand, I stared, panic-stricken, back at Daniel.

'I'm leaving,' he said tersely. 'There's no way I'm putting you and Jamie at risk. If someone can break in here . . .'

He didn't need to say any more. I knew exactly what he meant. We were as much in danger as he was.

'But how did they get in?' I asked. 'The door isn't damaged, and I'm positive I locked it when we went out. I remember dropping the kcy and having to brush the sand off before I did.'

'With an old door like this, it's easy. A credit card or anything thin can slip the lock.'

Something else that Daniel remembers, I thought uneasily. 'If you do,' I said slowly. 'And they come back . . .'

His mouth tightened. 'Becca, we don't know what I'm involved in, but it's obviously something very nasty. If anything happened to you . . . because of me . . . my life would be even more unbearable.'

'We'll tell the police—ask for protection.'

'Do you think it'll do any good? I can't see them parking an armed guard outside the door, can you?'

'Just ring them, Daniel,' I begged. 'We can't

just sit here, waiting.'

Listening to his side of the telephone conversation, it didn't sound encouraging, but when he came back into the room, he said, 'They're sending someone over.'

My breath sighed out with relief and I felt my body relax a little. 'But I still think I should leave here.'

'Don't!' I begged. 'Whoever did this won't know you've gone, and if they come back . . .'

'If I stay and they come back, it could be even worse.'

'I'd rather face that, than be on my own.'

He put both his hands round mine and gripped them tightly. 'All I've done is bring you trouble, Becca. You must wish so many times that you'd left me in the sea that night to drown.'

'No, Daniel,' I said quietly. 'There's no way I'll ever do that.'

'Matthew says there be a visitor coming soon, Mummy. Can we all have a picnic on the beach? It's very sunny.'

The back of my neck prickled. Matthew says . . . Was this another ominous warning?

'No, darling. We're going to stay indoors, but we can still have a picnic, if you want to. We'll lay the cloth on the floor and all sit round.'

Jamie glowered at me. 'You can't have picnics in houses, Mummy. Picnics are for outside. I don't want to stay indoors. I want to have a picnic on the beach.'

'Well, you're not going to,' I snapped, and saw his bottom lip quiver at the anger in my voice.

Daniel came and sat on his heels beside the little boy. 'Let's pretend we're in a cave.'

'Like smugglers and pirates when they've found treasure?' Jamie asked eagerly.

'Just like smugglers and pirates when they found treasure,' Daniel agreed. 'We'll pull all the curtains to keep out the daylight and pile some money in the middle of the tablecloth.'

'Smugglers and pirates wouldn't have a tablecloth,' Jamie told him firmly. 'Not in a cave.'

Daniel rubbed his chin and I could see he was trying not to smile. 'No, I suppose they wouldn't. We could pretend that little coffee table was a rock and use that.'

'If we had our picnic outside, we could use a real rock.'

'Yes, but then it wouldn't be like in a cave, would it, Jamie?'

'All right then, we'll pretend. What do smugglers and pirates eat, Daniel? I know, I'll ask Matthew.'

He ran across to the window-seat and I watched his head nod to and fro, before he came back to where Daniel sat on the floor.

'Could be pasties, or a bit of bread and cheese. Nice drop of wine, if there be a good haul. Couple of pilchards, mebbe.' His voice changed. 'Have we got any of those, Mummy?'

'How about tuna sandwiches, crisps and a banana?' I suggested, going into the kitchen.

Jamie wrinkled his nose and sighed. 'S'pose that'll have to do.'

I was mixing the tuna into mayonnaise when a fierce rapping on the front door made me drop the fork in panic. Daniel was on his feet instantly, and had picked up Jamie and bundled him into the kitchen, quickly closing the door behind him.

With my arms tightly round my son, I held my breath, waiting. I listened to Daniel's footsteps cross the other room into the hall, and his voice call out, 'Who is it?' but couldn't hear the reply.

'Mummy! You're squashing me,' Jamie protested.

'Stay still, darling!'

'Why?'

'Ssh!'

'Are we still pretending?'

'Yes,' I said quickly. 'It might be someone trying to catch the smugglers and pirates, so we must be very quiet.'

'Do they want to steal the smugglers' and pirates' treasure?'

'Yes,' I whispered.

He leaned his head into my waist and my arms tightened more closely round him. 'Becca!' Daniel was calling my name.

Warily, I opened the kitchen door a crack

and peered out into the darkened room, and then my heart gave a somersault.

Tim, my ex-husband, was standing there.

'What are you doing here?' I demanded, and couldn't prevent the coldness in my voice. 'I thought you were in New Zealand—with your new wife and family.'

Giving Daniel a sideways glance, Tim said, 'Can we speak alone?'

'It's OK, Becca, I'll take Jamie into the kitchen and make him that sandwich.'

When they were gone, I pulled back the curtains, letting sunshine brighten the room, then turned to Tim.

'So what are you doing here?'

'It hasn't worked out, Becca. I'm back in England now. For good.'

'You mean New Zealand hasn't worked out for you all?'

'No, Becca, my marriage to Lisa.'

I sank down on the window-seat, then smiled as the thought crossed my mind that I might be sitting on Matthew.

'It's not funny, Becca!' Tim's tone was sharp.

'I'm sorry, Tim, but this is all rather a shock. Why have you come here?'

He bent over me, one hand tilting my chin so that I had to look at him. 'Because I want you back, of course. Why else do you think I'm here? We should never have split up. We made a terrible mistake.'

66

I jerked my chin away. 'You made the mistake, not me, Tim. I never wanted our marriage to end. You know that only too well. I fought against it in every way. But, no. Lisa was all you wanted in life. You told me so many times. Your soul-mate. The one woman in the world for you.'

His lips tightened. 'I was wrong. I realise that now. You're the one women I want, Becca. And now we can be together again. Make a new start. You, me—and Jamie.'

Only weeks ago those words were all I ever longed to hear. To know that Tim still wanted me. But now . . .

The man I'd loved for so long was here, asking me to go back to him.

No, not asking me, but taking it for granted that I would. That we could forget everything that had happened and start again.

With no mention that he loved me.

I looked up into his dark eyes. Eyes that once had made my whole body weak with desire for him. Once, but now the magic had gone. He could have been a total stranger.

'Go and pack your stuff, darling. I've hired a car and parked it further up that dreadful track. No way was I going to damage it, bringing it right down here. What a place to live!' He smiled. 'I've booked into a hotel near Castle Beach in Falmouth. Hurry up then, Becca. We don't want to hang around here all day, do we?'

I turned my head to gaze out through the salt-hazed window. The tide was starting to come in, white-capped waves rising high, before thundering down to race up the beach. I could hear the faint drag of shingle as each one retreated. Little brown wading birds delved their beaks along the shoreline, darting to and fro. Gulls drifted lazily, high in the sky above. Far out to sea, a white sail billowed.

'I'm not going anywhere, Tim.'

'What do you mean? Not going.'

'Just that, Tim. You walked out of my life two years ago. For me, that's final.'

'But what about Jamie? He's my son.'

'And you've made no attempt to see or be with him in all that time. You had a new family, you said. It wouldn't be fair on them. Like me, Jamie has learnt to live without you. I doubt he even remembers you.'

'You can't do this to me, Becca.'

'But I am, Tim.'

'Because of this man you're living with?'

I frowned. 'I'm not living with anyone.'

Tim raised one eyebrow and jerked his head sideways. 'In the kitchen? Making my son a sandwich?'

I laughed. 'Daniel? I'm not living with Daniel.'

'Oh no?' he said. 'Then what's he doing here? He seems to be very much at home.'

'You obviously haven't read the newspapers, Tim.'

'That's not surprising. I only arrived in England yesterday. And came straight down here this morning. At least I knew where you were living.'

'And where you were supposed to be sending me maintenance,' I observed coldly. 'If you had read a paper, you'd have known that I rescued Daniel from the sea.'

'So why's he still here?'

I shook my head. 'It's a long story.'

'I've plenty of time.'

'Not long enough,' I replied, rising slowly to my feet. 'Anyway, you're in a hurry to get back to civilisation. And we've nothing more to say to each other. Goodbye, Tim.'

'You can't just . . .' he began.

'Oh, but I can,' I replied, going into the hall and opening the front door.

'You haven't heard the end of this, Becca.'

Silently, I closed it behind him—before I let myself cry.

CHAPTER NINE

As the door closed, I heard Daniel come out of the kitchen. 'Oh, Becca!' he said, seeing my tears, and I turned to bury my face into the warmth of his shoulder, feeling his fingers smooth lightly down the back of my neck and his arm draw me closer while sobs tore through my body, and there was no way I could stop them.

'Do you love him so much?' He whispered the words into my hair.

I raised my head, seeing my own pain reflected in his eyes. 'Not any more,' I murmured. 'But . . .'

His hand moved gently across my cheek, brushing away tears. 'But once you did—and that makes it even worse, doesn't it? To know that love has died. It's like a bereavement. A final ending. I loved my wife, Jane, very much, so, in a way, I think I can understand a little of how you're feeling.' Pulling away, I stared at him. 'You can remember her then?'

He nodded. 'Yes, quite clearly. She was a tall, strongly-built girl. A great sailor—which is why her father bought that boat. And she loved sailing it. We both did. We often crossed to Brittany—with my brother.'

'Barry?'

He frowned and I saw lines of tension draw at his mouth. 'Yes,' he said slowly, and his body stiffened, his jaw hardening. 'My brother, Barry.'

'Mummy! Can I come back now? I've eaten my sandwich.' Jamie appeared through the kitchen door. 'Was that man my daddy?'

'Yes, darling,' I said.

'Where's he gone? He didn't say hello to me. Or goodbye.'

'He had to go, Jamie.'

70

'To see those other children? The ones he lives with in that other country, 'stead of living with us?'

'I don't know where he's gone, darling.'

Jamie slipped his arms round my neck and kissed my cheek. 'Never mind, Mummy. We've got Daniel to love us now, haven't we? You won't go away and leave us, will you, Daniel?'

'Would you like a banana, Jamie?' I said quickly, trying to divert his conversation to safer ground.

'Is that what pirates eat?'

'Most days,' Daniel replied, smiling at me as he took the little boy's hand and guided him towards the kitchen. 'Let's go and finish our picnic, shall we?'

'Don't tell my Daddy about that treasure, will you? Matthew says someone might come and steal it when we're asleep.'

Matthew says . . .

My skin prickled—those words terrifying me yet again.

Scarlet rays of sun were fingering across the sea that evening before the police inspector's car came slowly down the track and stopped by the cottage.

'Had a bit of trouble, have you?'

Silently, Daniel handed him the sheet of paper we'd found on the hall floor when we returned earlier in the day.

'You lost the goods. Now you owe me,' the Inspector read out. 'You know who wrote this,

71

Mr Trevose?'

'Of course, I don't!'

'You know what it refers to though.'

'Presumably the stuff you found on board my boat.'

The Inspector ran his tongue over his teeth as if searching for some missed fragment of food.

'Looks like it. Best take this back and have it checked for finger-prints.'

He scratched his nose. 'Be covered in yours, of course, seeing as how you've both picked it up and read it.'

'And yours,' I added.

'On the hall floor, you say?' he asked Daniel, ignoring me. 'Pushed under the door, was it?'

'No, the door was open when we came back.'

'Forgot to lock it?'

'No, I definitely locked it,' I said. 'I dropped the key and had to brush sand off, before I put it in the lock.'

'No sign of any damage,' he commented, starting to move towards his car.

I stepped in front of him, blocking his way. 'Someone broke into my home, Inspector. If they did it once, they can do it again. What are you going to do about it?'

He pushed out his lower lip. 'No damage done. Nothing stolen.'

'I have a young child, Inspector.'

Opening the car door, he settled himself into the seat, stretched the belt over his stomach, and switched on the engine. 'Any problem—dial 999.'

Carefully reversing, with a spatter of tiny stones the car sped away up the track.

'A lot of good that did then,' Daniel said, a muscle twitching in his taut cheek.

'There might be finger-prints on it,' I suggested.

'Underneath all of ours? I doubt they'd be very clear. And anyway, unless it's a known criminal, they won't be on record.'

'You know who left that note, don't you?'

'Of course I don't, Becca. How could I?'

'If this memory loss is all a bluff . . .'

He put both hands on my shoulders. 'Becca, believe me. It isn't. There's no way I would lie to you. Bits are there, I admit that. But the rest . . . I really can't remember. I only wish I could.'

'I'm so frightened, Daniel,' I whispered.

'And it's all my fault,' he groaned, leaning his forehead against mine. 'It would have been so much better if I'd drowned that night. None of this would have affected you.'

'Don't say that, Daniel! If you hadn't come into my life . . .'

My voice died away.

His hands slid slowly from my shoulders, up the length of my neck, until they cupped my face, lifting my chin, so that I was looking deep into his eyes.

'If I hadn't come into your life, Becca?' His gaze questioned mine.

But there was no way I could tell him and I closed my eyes, not wanting them to reveal the answer.

Stepping backwards, I let my face slip from his fingers, regretting every movement.

Abruptly, he turned and went indoors.

It was hours before I slept that night, my mind twisting and turning. I'd learnt so much about Daniel that day, as more of his memory returned. But what would it finally reveal?

And Tim had come back. Something I'd wanted for so many months. Was it really too late for us to be together? For Jamie's sake?

He'd caused me so much heartache, deserting us like that, for someone else. Would I ever be able to trust him again? Did I want to?

When I finally slept, my dreams were nightmares. Darkness. A sea where huge waves rose high, before crashing down in a roar like thunder. First one, then two, heads appeared and disappeared as each wave descended.

Daniel.

Tim.

Which should I save? With the next wave, a third surfaced—and I saw it was Jamie.

I could feel myself being swept away from them, back towards the shore; my arms

74

desperately flailing, my breath tearing at my chest, the pain in my throat as I tried to call out.

The ache was still there when I woke, shaking with terror. Breathlessly I lay, with sunshine filtering in through the bedroom curtains, making my body relax. Just a dream. Nothing more, I told myself. But even so, I pulled on my dressing-gown and ran into Jamie's room.

He lay, one hand curled above his head on the pillow, the other resting near his mouth. Even at four years old he still sometimes sucked his thumb to go to sleep. Tucked beside him, so that only his flattened face showed above the covers, was a faded blue rabbit, fur thin from too many sessions in the washing machine.

I tiptoed out, and went downstairs to make a mug of tea.

As I crossed the hall, I could see Daniel through the open door, asleep face-down on the sofa, duvet trailing the floor. The scars and bruises on his sun-tanned back had faded a little, but must still be painful, although he never mentioned them.

His honey-coloured hair was thick, peaking to a point just below the nape of his neck, and half-covering his ears. Surprisingly dark stubble reached down from them to the firm line of his jaw. One arm was buried under his pillow, while the other touched the carpet.

As if sensing my presence, he twisted his head sideways on the pillow, then with a sudden movement turned on to his back. Swiftly, I went into the kitchen.

'Shall we continue the search for your past today, Daniel?' I asked, as we finished breakfast.

Spreading marmalade on to a slice of toast, he bit into it. 'All we seemed to do yesterday was reach a dead end.'

'No, we didn't! That woman—Hannah—in the coffee house knew you. And then there's Peter Carrick, your father-in-law. If we go to Feock again, he might be home. Or, if he's away, maybe one of his neighbours can tell us where he's gone and when he'll be back. You can't just give up now, Daniel.'

He picked up his mug of coffee and, with troubled eyes, looked at me over its rim. 'I'm not sure I'm going to like the person I turn out to be.'

'You still have to know, Daniel,' I replied gently, my fingers brushing across the shoulder of his faded blue sweatshirt. 'Let's get this washed up and take a picnic with us. Loe Beach looked quite interesting with all those little boats.'

'Matthew says I mustn't go there,' Jamie announced, climbing down from the window-seat and coming back to the table.

'Then you'd better tell Matthew that you are and if he doesn't like it, it's just too bad,' I

76

replied firmly, piling our empty bowls into the sink and turning on the hot tap. I had enough to cope with, persuading Daniel, without an imaginary friend creating problems.

'But, Mummy . . .'

'No more arguments, Jamie. Just fetch your anorak. We're leaving in five minutes.'

Now that I knew the way, it was an easy journey, and soon we were driving down the narrow, twisting hill that led to Peter Carrick's house. Yet again, the place appeared deserted and, having wandered round the overgrown garden and peered in through the salt-crusted windows, we gave up and returned to the gate.

An elderly man with a very wet spaniel was climbing up from the beach, as we came out into the lane, and he stopped to wait until we reached him.

'Looking for Peter?'

'Yes,' I said. 'Is he away?'

'Hospital. Heart. Not been fit for quite a while. Refused to see the quack though.'

He gave Daniel a searching glance. 'Seen you before, haven't I? Used to come and stay with Peter? Married to his daughter, weren't you? Lovely girl. Sad thing, that.'

Bending over the dog for a moment, he clipped on its lead. 'Come on then, Gertie. Time for lunch. Nice to have met you again, young man.'

It was only a small beach, sheltered by rocks, with trees growing right down to the water's edge.

Little boats swung from their moorings, while a few larger ones were pulled up on to the tiny car park behind us.

A teenage boy stood, waist-deep, patiently teaching another to balance on a windsurf board, but from the constant splashing, he wasn't having a great deal of success.

Jamie watched, fascinated, as he chewed a crusty ham roll.

'Can I do that, Mummy?'

'One day. When you've learnt to swim properly.'

'Matthew says sailors don't learn to swim, 'cos it be better to drown when your ships be wrecked.'

Matthew says.

How I'd grown to dread those two words.

CHAPTER TEN

'Over to the hospital next?' I asked Daniel while we were putting the remains of our picnic back into the cool-box.

'To see Peter Carrick? We can try, I suppose, but it depends on just how ill he is, whether they'll let us.'

'Well, if we don't try, we'll never know, will we?' I said, locking the boot of the car. 'Come on, Jamie.'

It didn't take long to reach the outskirts of the town and turn off the main road to reach the hospital. Once there, we found the reception area and, deciding a direct approach was the only way, I asked which ward Peter Carrick was in.

'Are you a relative?'

'I'm his son-in-law,' Daniel said, quickly interrupting.

The cool gaze of the receptionist challenged him. 'Mr Carrick's son-in-law visited him earlier this afternoon.'

'Well, I'm another one.'

She frowned down at Jamie. 'You can't take the little boy into the ward. He'll have to remain here in reception with your wife.'

I looked anxiously at Daniel. I wanted to be with him to hear what Peter Carrick had to say, but I couldn't leave Jamie on his own.

'Don't worry,' he said. 'I'll be all right.'

After he'd gone up in the lift, I sat on a leather bench and picked up one of the well-thumbed magazines. Jamie had already discovered the children's corner and was tipping a box of Lego on to the floor.

'Mr Carrick's son-in-law visited him earlier this afternoon . . .' That's what the receptionist said. Could it have been Barry Trevose, Daniel's brother? And, if so, why the pretence? Surely Peter Carrick would realise the difference?

But the two brothers were very much alike.

I'd almost been fooled when I saw Barry for the first time. And as for the man Jamie and I had seen in the crowded town that time—I still didn't know which of them it was.

I watched the minute hand on the wall clock move round the dial. Five. Ten. Fifteen. What could Daniel and his father-in-law be saying to each other for so long? If only I was there with them.

The lift door opened and two elderly ladies stepped out, one helping the other who was dabbing at her eyes with a handkerchief.

'It's only to be expected at his age, Evelyn,' I heard her say as they passed my seat. 'No-one can go on for ever, dear.'

A trolley piled with cups and saucers rattled down the corridor and was wheeled into the lift. Jamie glanced at it hopefully before returning to whatever he was constructing.

Twenty minutes had passed now. Where was Daniel? And then I began to wonder whether Barry Trevose was still with Peter Carrick. If the two brothers had met . . .

'I'm thirsty, Mummy.' Jamie was shaking my knee. 'There's a machine over there and that lady put some money in and a drink came out. Can I try?'

Following him to the dispenser, I studied the instructions, put in a pound coin and pressed one of the picture buttons. With a thump, a carton of orange juice rolled down the chute. Jamie pounced on it, tugging off the

80

straw and pushing it into the top, sending up a fountain of liquid.

'Don't press the sides like that, darling,' I warned.

When I turned to go back to my seat, Daniel was stepping out of the lift, and I read distress in his eyes.

'Are you OK?" I said, putting my hand on his arm.

He nodded wearily. 'Let's get out of here. I hate these places.'

Back at the car, I strapped Jamie into his seat and then spoke to Daniel. 'What did Peter Carrick have to say?'

'Not much. He's in a very poor way, but kept asking why I'd come back. I thought at first he meant why had I come back to Cornwall, and tried to tell him about the boat being wrecked. Eventually, I realised he was asking why I'd come back again today. I explained to him that this was my first visit.'

Daniel eased the seatbelt away from his shoulder and I guessed it was rubbing on one of the bruises.

'And then he started asking for Jane. Where was she? Why wasn't she with me? He kept repeating that I'd promised to bring her and was becoming quite agitated.

'So much so that a nurse came over and suggested I leave, but Peter insisted I stay. I just didn't know what to do. He's obviously in a very confused state.'

'Do you think it was Barry who visited him earlier?' I said. 'But if so, why pretend to be you? And why promise to bring Jane? How could he be so cruel to her father, knowing that she's dead? What else do you think he said? And why visit him in the first place?'

'Oh, Becca, if only I knew.' Daniel gave an exasperated sigh. 'Everything's growing more and more complicated. I just wish it would end.'

As we drove down the track to the cottage, my heart began to beat faster, remembering the previous time we'd made the journey. Stopping the car outside, I anxiously studied the front door but this time it was definitely shut.

Even so, I unlocked it cautiously, stepping back as I pushed it open, but to my relief there was no note lying on the hall floor.

'Mummy! You've forgotten my ice cream! You promised.'

'Don't worry, Jamie,' Daniel said, joining us. 'There was a van parked near the top of the cliff. I'll walk up there and buy some.'

'We could all go in the car,' I suggested, not wanting to be on my own.

'It's OK. It won't take five minutes and I could do with a walk. Might clear my head a little. Choc ice, Jamie?'

'Yes, please!' He picked up his red plastic bucket from the step. 'Can Matthew and me go and look for treasure, Mummy?'

'No, darling. Stay near the cottage, where I can see you from the window, while I'm making our meal. The tide's coming in so I don't want you anywhere near the sea.'

'All right, Mummy. Matthew and me'll be just here. There's some nice sand to build castles. Matthew says he won't let no harm come to me.'

Through the hazed glass I watched him fill his bucket, then tip out the shaped sand, his mouth moving in silent conversation. Handfuls of tiny stones and bits of shell were held out as if for approval, before being studded over the castle walls.

How long will it be, I wondered as I shredded lettuce into a bowl, until Matthew is forgotten? The telephone suddenly trilled in the lounge and, wiping my wet hands on a towel, I went to answer it. A voice—whether a man's or woman's I couldn't tell as it was so faint—murmured something.

'Could you speak up, please? I can't hear you.'

The murmur came again, slightly louder, but still the words were indistinguishable.

'I'm sorry, but . . .' Before I could say more, there was a click and silence. At the same time, the door opened and Daniel returned, carrying a paper bag.

'Jamie! Come and get your ice cream. It's starting to melt.'

'He's outside,' I said, taking tomatoes from

83

the fridge.

'Where?'

'Just there . . .' I glanced out through the window, seeing only an upturned red bucket and heap of scattered sand where the castles had been.

'Jamie!' Panic caught at my throat, thinning my voice. 'Jamie!'

My feet flew over the beach to where growing waves crept in, nudging a thin line of seaweed on to the sand and shingle.

'Jamie!' I swung round to Daniel. 'He was there only minutes ago. I could see him through the window. And then the phone rang . . .'

'Who was it?' Daniel's tone was urgent.

'I don't know. I couldn't hear. Oh, Daniel, he can't . . .'

'Go back indoors, Becca. Ring the police. I'll keep looking. He's probably just wandered away.' But I knew, from the tone of his voice, he didn't believe that.

The Inspector arrived surprisingly fast. A police woman accompanied him. That only increased my fears.

'This phone call,' he said, eyeing me sharply. 'You're sure you couldn't hear what was being said?'

'No!'

'Could be a wrong number, I suppose . . .' He scratched the side of his cheek with a nicotine-stained finger. 'Or it could be a

84

method of distraction. Didn't see anyone on the beach, did you?'

I shook my head.

'Or on the track, Mr Trevose?' He leaned forward, his bloodshot eyes peering closely at Daniel. 'The boy could've followed you up to the ice cream van.'

'He didn't!' I shouted. 'I told you. Jamie was right outside here. Building sandcastles. You can see where he was playing.'

It was then I heard the drone of a helicopter, growing louder, and looking through the open door saw it weave its way, crab-like, round the cliffs and begin to circle over the sea, getting lower and lower.

'No!' The wail of anguish tore through my lips and Daniel's arms closed round me, holding me against his chest, smoothing his hand over my hair. 'He will be all right, Becca. They will find him.'

'But what will they find?' I sobbed.

It became worse as the hours passed. Divers in a rubber dinghy came racing past the rocks and swept into the cove. I watched its sides dip as they jumped into the water and disappeared, black heads surfacing at intervals, before vanishing again.

Floodlights lined the beach as the sky darkened, suddenly blazing out to silhouette figures moving along the shoreline.

And all I could do was wait, my whole body trembling, trying to stop the thoughts seethed in my mind.

Matthew says he won't let no harm come to me.

Those were the last words Jamie had spoken.

Matthew says . . .

I looked across at the window-seat and strangely my body began to relax. Everything Matthew said, had come true.

The shipwreck.

Finding treasure—and to some those drugs were treasure.

Visitors coming—Tim?

Danger. We'd certainly had plenty of that.

Was Matthew just a figment of my son's imagination, or . . .

Matthew says he won't let no harm come to me.

I forced my mind to concentrate on those words. I had to. There was nothing else I could do.

The police woman kept making tea in the kitchen, bringing it out in mugs on a plastic tray. Mine, I noticed, was always sweet. I hate sugar in my tea. Maybe she thought it would help. I couldn't tell her.

She was carrying in yet another tray, when the Inspector came indoors. Daniel's arm tensed round my shoulders.

'Have to give up now, 'till morning, I'm ~raid. Tide's way out and it's far too dark. I ~w it's difficult, but try and get some sleep, my dear,' he said in a surprisingly gentle voice, and I saw his face was lined with exhaustion. Even the bags under his eyes seemed to have doubled in size. 'We'll start again as soon as it gets light.'

One by one the floodlights went out. Voices died away into the distance. I heard the splutter of an engine and guessed it was the frogman's dinghy. The helicopter had gone some time before, either called to another emergency or needing to re-fuel.

Daniel and I were left in silence. 'Jamie's not in the sea,' I said. 'I'm sure of that.'

'How can you be?' Daniel sounded desolate.

'That phone call. It was too much of a coincidence, coming at exactly the same moment Jamie disappeared. Someone with a mobile phone could have made it, from outside here. And those sandcastles. Jamie wouldn't knock them down like that. You know he loves decorating them with shells and stones, and then they stay there for days. That's what he was doing when I was watching him through the window.

'So where . . .'

'It's Tim. His way of getting me back. Phone the Inspector, Daniel. Tell him.'

'There is another possibility, Becca.'

'No,' I insisted. 'It's Tim. He's taken Jamie.'

'Becca! Listen to me. Whoever sent th note . . .' He paused and I saw his mo tighten.

'No.'

'It's something we've got to face, Becca. Whatever I'm mixed up in . . . People like that . . .'

I couldn't prevent the bitterness in my voice as I swung round to face him.

'People like you, isn't that what you really mean?'

CHAPTER ELEVEN

'Don't say that, Becca. Please,' Daniel implored. 'I only hope I'm wrong and if anyone has taken Jamie, it is his father.' I put my hands over my face, trying to keep back the tears, but it was no use.

'He's such a little boy, Daniel,' I sobbed, my whole body shaking. 'He doesn't even know Tim any more. To him he's a complete stranger now.'

My back straightened as another thought struck me. 'Why didn't he cry out, Daniel? He was right outside the door. I was only in the lounge for a minute or so. Why didn't I hear something?'

Furiously, I grabbed Daniel's arm and shook it. 'You must have seen something. There must have been a vehicle. It would have travel up and down the track. There's no r way to reach the cottage. Think, Daniel!

Did you see anything at all?'

He shook his head despairingly. 'I saw nothing, Becca, and no-one. Just the ice cream van.'

I frowned at him. 'That's never been up there before, has it?'

'Not that I've noticed, but they do stop anywhere. The driver might have parked for a quiet five minutes.'

'We need to speak to the Inspector. He's so convinced that . . .' My voice choked and it took moments before I could say the next words. '. . . that Jamie has . . . drowned.'

I leaned my head into Daniel's shoulder, needing the comfort of his arms holding me. He lips moved against my hair, and his voice was full of anger as he said, 'What have I done to you, Becca? Why, oh why, did I have to destroy your life, in an attempt to save mine?'

Someone else answered Daniel's call to the police station. The Inspector wasn't there, but a message would be passed to him, he was told. Until then, we could only wait.

I sat on Jamie's bed, cuddling the little blue rabbit, remembering it was only a few hours since I'd seen my child asleep there. Where was he now?

He'd never been away from me before. I'd always been there to tuck him under th covers, read him a story, give him a goodn kiss, before tiptoeing out of the room whe eyelids drooped and he drifted into sleep

If he woke first in the morning, I'd find him snuggled under my duvet, blue rabbit clutched under one pyjama arm, his cheeks rosy with warmth, fair hair tousled, his mouth smiling with the joy of seeing me.

Now he must be terrified.

I heard footsteps on the stairs and Daniel appeared in the doorway, holding two mugs.

'Oh, not more tea!' I wailed. 'Why does everyone think it's the answer to all troubles?'

'I need to do something Becca, even if it's only making tea. I hate this sitting around waiting. I want to be out there, searching. But where, even to start?'

The mattress sank as he sat down beside me on the bed and I took one of the mugs, wrapping my fingers round it, watching a cluster of tiny bubbles on the surface of the liquid slowly disappear.

Picking up the little blue rabbit. Daniel stroked his finger over its flattened nose.

'When he was tiny, Jamie always kissed it goodnight,' I told him. 'I think, secretly, he still does, which accounts for the squashed nose. Once it had black woollen whiskers, but those vanished years ago. It was a first birthday present. Tim bought it.'

'It must have been very hard for you when Tim left.'

I nodded, my throat tightening. expected. I had no idea. He told me I was otted with Jamie that he felt neglected.'

I shrugged. 'He was probably right. But I thought he loved the baby as much as I did. He was always buying him toys. Far too many. We argued about that at times. I didn't want our son to grow up, showered with everything he demanded.'

Taking the little rabbit from Daniel, I tucked it under Jamie's duvet, so that it would be waiting for him when . . .

My eyes blurred and I felt Daniel's fingers grip round mine. 'I discovered later that Tim's affair with Lisa began over a year before Jamie was born. With young children of her own, I don't know how she found the time. I think her husband was just as surprised as I was when they announced they were leaving us.'

'So Tim and Lisa married and moved to New Zealand?'

'Yes. A fresh start, he said. Tim decided it wasn't fair to his new family if he remained in touch with Jamie and me, so that was that.

'He walked out of our life for ever.

'You can imagine what a bombshell it was when he turned up here out of the blue.'

'How did he know where to find you?'

'He has this address to send maintenance— for his son. It came—spasmodically. Living in New Zealand, I wasn't sure he would bother.'

'Now that he's returned . . .' Daniel's voice ended in an unspoken question.

'I'm not going back to him,' I said firmly.

'Not even for Jamie's sake?'

Daniel's words jolted through me, bringing me back to reality. Jamie.

'It is Tim who's taken him, isn't it, Daniel?' I said. 'Please say it's Tim. I can't bear the thought of anyone else . . .'

But the only answer Daniel gave was to hold me close, his cheek resting against mine.

Despite all the anguish, exhaustion eventually caught up with me and I dozed, waking to find myself lying on Jamie's pillow, his duvet covering me. Sleepily, I raised my head and for a few brief seconds everything was forgotten—until the horror came rushing back and I sat up.

Through the diamond-paned window I saw the horizon, bordered red, daylight growing, and heard the thin whine of an engine as the frogmen's dinghy bounced over the sea, plumes of spray curling up on either side, before the sound cut out and it bobbed gently in the cove.

Already rescue vehicles were arriving on the shingle and people moved between them, voices muted. I closed my eyes, trying to push away the rising panic that was threatening to overwhelm me.

Jamie isn't dead.

I kept repeating the words in my head like a mantra, trying to make myself believe them. A dumpy figure separated from one of the groups and began to walk across the beach towards the cottage.

The Inspector.

What was he doing there? Hasn't he received the message? Why wasn't he searching for Tim—and Jamie?

Pushing back my untidy tangle of hair, I ran down the stairs to find him talking with Daniel in the kitchen. Their conversation stopped when I appeared and reading the expression on their faces, my stomach lurched.

'What's happened?'

The Inspector pulled a chair out from the kitchen table. 'I think you've best sit down.'

'What's happened?' My head twisted from one to the other. 'Tell me!'

'There was another note,' Daniel said. 'I found it earlier, here on the table.'

I stared back at him, disbelieving. 'The table?' I echoed. 'But . . . you were sleeping in the next room. Why didn't you hear something?'

Suspicion filtered into my mind as I looked at him, stubble darkening his chin, hair ruffled.

'You wrote it, Daniel! You put it there.'

My hands reached out, clutching his sweatshirt, my fists pounding into his chest as I sobbed: 'What have you done with Jamie? Where is he? Daniel, please, please tell me where he is.'

He caught my wrists, grasping them firmly, and I saw his own eyes were brimming with emotion. 'Believe me, Becca! I've done nothing. I promise you.'

Still holding on to me, he turned to the Inspector. 'I think you'd better let her read that note.'

Delving into an inner pocket of his jacket, the Inspector produced a plastic bag with a sheet of paper inside and handed it to me.

'Careful! Don't take it out!'

Holding it with trembling fingers, I read the printed words.

ONE OUTSTANDING DEBT IN EXCHANGE FOR ONE CHILD BETTER MAKE IT QUICK, HADN'T YOU?

The room wavered and, like a thick cloak, darkness folded over me, the floor rushing up.

I was lying on the lounge sofa when I opened my eyes, the young police woman bending over me. Any moment now, I thought, she'll produce a mug of tea.

Pushing her arm away, I sat up, my head swirling as I took in the meaning of her words.

'. . . before they leave . . .'

An ambulance had been there, on the beach, waiting. For what? I wouldn't let myself even think of the answer.

'What's happening?' I asked, swinging my legs down from the sofa. 'Have they found Jamie?'

'The sea search has been called off. We're concentrating on other areas now. You'd best stay there, resting. You're still a funny colour. 'll go and make you some tea.'

'I don't want any tea,' I stormed. 'I want to

94

know what's happening.'

She gave me a despairing look. 'I don't know anything more myself. My instructions are to stay with you and they'll keep me informed of any further developments.'

'Where's Daniel?' I asked, glancing out of the window to where a procession of vehicles was winding slowly up the track.

'The Inspector's taken him in.'

A dull feeling crept over me. So my suspicions about Daniel were right, after all.

I'd wanted so much to believe Daniel, but now I realised that everything had been one big lie. Maybe, right at the beginning, when I dragged him from the sea, he really had lost his memory.

At what stage it returned, and he decided it was to his advantage to keep up the pretence, I just don't know. All I knew was that I'd trusted him, but not any more.

He was part of the criminal underworld—peopled by those who didn't care how or whom they hurt. People who would snatch a little child—my child—to gain what they wanted.

At least the Inspector had seen through Daniel's pretence, but would he be able to find Jamie?

Daniel must know who these people were. He worked with them, transporting drugs in his boat. If it hadn't been wrecked in the storm and the cargo found and confiscated by th

95

police, Daniel would have made a lot of money for them, so it wasn't surprising they wanted repayment.

Oh, why was I the one to save him that night and then be foolish enough to let him stay here? Why didn't I refuse?

But Daniel was clever. That loss of memory. He made it all so convincing. And I wanted to believe him. How could he lie to me like that?

And what about his brother? Was he involved? Daniel said they sailed the boat together. But that was when Jane, his wife, was alive. Or was that also a lie?

And yet the waitress in the coffee house remembered Jane—and Daniel. She knew about her death, too. So at least that was true. She'd been the one who mentioned Jane's father, Peter Carrick.

Then there was the conversation Daniel said he had in the hospital with his father-in-law. He made it sound as though Peter Carrick was in a very confused state. After a heart attack, perhaps he was, or had their conversation been entirely different? Was Peter Carrick also involved in some way? Were they really arguing about that?

The receptionist did say that a son-in-law had been to see him and I assumed it was Barry Trevose, pretending to be Daniel. But was it? Why would he visit?

Perhaps both brothers were mixed up in this smuggling racket, with Peter Carrick. If so, does that mean Barry kidnapped my son to put pressure on Daniel?

My mind whirled with unanswered questions. And all this time Jamie was still missing, with no-one being any closer to finding him.

'They've arranged for a doctor to call in to give you a sedative. Calm you down a little.' The policewoman came back into the lounge, carrying a tray.

'I don't want a sedative,' I stormed, pushing away the mug she held out to me, sending a stream of hot tea cascading on to the carpet. 'I want my son back.'

'You mustn't get so upset,' she said, standing the mug back on the tray and dabbing the floor with a tissue. 'I appreciate it must be very worrying for you, but we really don't have a great deal to go on. You are quite sure he was only out of your sight for a few minutes?'

'Positive!'

'Children can be extremely quick, you know. And little boys of that age are full of curiosity. He liked playing on the beach, didn't he? Not unusual for him to wander off on his own?'

'I've told you,' I said through clenched teeth. 'Jamie was right outside the window, building sandcastles. I saw him decorating them with bits of shell and stones. He had a handful of them.'

'When he'd used those up, he'd have gone to find some more though, wouldn't he? Alor the shoreline?'

I could see where her questions were leading. 'Jamie wouldn't knock the castles down—and you saw for yourself that they were trampled and scattered. He always left them. It would take days before they finally disintegrated. Anyway, you read the note.'

Seeing the expression on her face, a horrible idea hit me. 'You believe Daniel or I wrote it, don't you? That we're in this together?'

'It has been known.'

'How can you even think I'd do anything to harm my son?' I demanded. 'I adore him.'

'But you have gone out of your way to help Daniel Trevose. I can see that he is a very attractive man, and love can play strange tricks on people.'

'You think I'd harm my son because of Daniel?'

She took a sip of her tea and regarded me steadily over the rim of the mug. 'As I said before, it has been known.'

'Well, you're quite, quite wrong,' I retorted angrily.

The radio clipped to her uniform spluttered and she hurried into the kitchen to answer it. There was no way I was staying to wait for her return. Slipping into the hall, I tugged open the front door and ran over the shingle to where my car was parked.

Dragging the keys from the pocket of my ans, I unlocked the door, but as I struggled to start the engine, I saw her rush out of the cottage.

Why does a car always refuse to start first time, when you're in a hurry? Desperately, I pumped my foot on the accelerator, dreading I'd flood the engine, before it roared into life and, with gravel spattered from under the tyres, began to climb the track. In the rear mirror, I could see her speaking rapidly into the radio.

Now I was the hunted one.

The main roads wouldn't be safe, so I turned off down a series of narrow, twisting lanes, arched into tunnels by windswept trees. I had no idea where I was going.

All I wanted was to escape from the questioning eyes of that policewoman—yet, by doing so, I'd probably only confirmed her suspicion that Daniel and I had harmed Jamie in some way.

From the wording of that last note, it was clear that Tim hadn't taken Jamie. I only wished he had. Tim wouldn't hurt his own son.

Fear tore through me, knotting my stomach. My fingers clenched so tightly round the steering wheel that I almost drove into the high grass bank as I spun round a corner. Slow down, I told myself. Slow down before you have an accident.

Passing a signpost, I realised I was on the road leading to Feock and Loe Beach. Wa some instinct taking me there? But, in such a

99

out of the way and quiet area, Peter Carrick's empty house would make an ideal place to hide a child.

Wisps of mist covered the windscreen with dampness as I grew nearer the sea and I flicked the wipers across, trying not to miss the turning. With the car parked on the little patch of muddy grass halfway down the hill, I stepped out into the cold air.

The wrought-iron gate to the house was pushed back into the hedge and I tried to remember whether we'd left it like that the previous day. Someone else, maybe a postman, could have called though, since then.

By going up the path, I would be visible if anyone was indoors, so I walked further up the lane, following the line of the hedge, until I came to another smaller gate leading to the back garden. The mist was much thicker now, swirling in from the sea like smoke, hiding the trees and prickling my skin.

I had to lean hard against the gate, forcing it open on to the overgrown lawn. Strands of wet grass soaked my jeans as I trampled through them, towards the house.

Again, it looked deserted. Getting closer, I peered through one of the windows, but my view was blocked by the high back of a sofa. The room seemed empty, but it was too gloomy in there for me to be sure. I needed to be inside.

A long, low, mournful sound echoed,

scaring me, until I realised it was the fog horn from the lighthouse at St Anthony Head, and continued my search for a way in.

I'd just found the back door, when something thumped against my back, almost knocking me over and I spun round, terrified.

'Gertie! Get down!'

Jumping up at me was a wet and very bedraggled spaniel, its paws leaving muddy trails down my anorak. 'I'm so sorry, my dear. She's getting deaf, you see. Can't hear a word I say.'

Peter Carrick's elderly neighbour came hurrying across the grass towards me, flapping the dog's lead in one hand.

'Gertie! Stand still, will you, and let me clip this on.'

He stood up again, red in the face, tugging the dog to one side. 'I do hope she hasn't ruined your jacket, my dear.'

'No, no. It'll brush off when it's dry.'

He peered at me from under bushy white eyebrows. 'You're the girl who was here the other day with Peter's son-in-law, aren't you? Any luck with seeing Peter?'

'Yes, Daniel visited him at the hospital.'

I thought quickly. 'Peter asked him to pick up a few things from the house. You don't know if anyone has a key, do you?'

'Key?'

He fished in the deep pocket of his duf coat and produced one dangling from a p

101

of string. 'Pop in every now and then to collect Peter's post. Don't like to leave it lying on the mat. Tells people the place is empty. Can't be too careful nowadays.'

I bent to stroke the spaniel's damp head. 'She's a lovely dog, isn't she?' I said, smiling up at the old man. 'I hardly like to ask this, but would it be possible to let me into the house, so that I can collect those things for Peter?'

'No trouble at all, my dear,' he said, leading the way round to the front door and fitting in the key. 'There you are. Just give it a slam when you come out. Locks itself.'

I stood on the mat inside the door, hardly able to believe my luck, watching as he marched off down the path and stopped at the gate to give a little salute, before disappearing into the mist.

The silence of the house closed round me. Now that I was there, I wasn't sure what to do. I wasn't even sure why I was there. If Peter Carrick, Barry and Daniel Trevose were all involved with smuggling, surely they wouldn't leave anything around to say so.

Swiftly I went from room to room. First, the one I'd seen through the window—a lounge with two big sofas and several armchairs covered in flowered chintz, faded along the backs from years of sunshine. Bookshelves ned every wall and I saw that most volumes re historical biographies, with a large ction on sailing and the Navy.

A heavy leather-topped desk with brass-handled drawers stood at one end and I pulled them out, one by one, not really knowing what I expected to find, but didn't dare spend time going through the papers and files that filled them.

Surprisingly, when I looked in, the kitchen was quite modern, almost clinical, with its white-fronted units, cooker, fridge/freezer, washing machine, drier and dishwasher neatly fitted.

I glanced at my watch. Any minute the neighbour might return to check whether I'd left yet. Upstairs all the bedroom doors were closed. The landing was very dark and the air felt chilly and damp. The back of my neck prickled as, cautiously, I reached out and opened the first door, revealing heavy mahogany furniture and a double bed heaped with blankets and a rose-pink eiderdown.

I moved on to the next room, slightly smaller, but with similar furnishings. In the third two single beds were ranged on either side, with a vanity unit between them and fitted whitewood wardrobes.

The final door opened into a bathroom, still in its original state—claw-foot bath, pedestal washbasin with dripping taps that had left a blue-green trail, and a toilet with wooden seat and china-handled chain dangling from an overhead cistern.

I turned away to close the door again, th

stopped as something caught my eye. Under the bath, screwed into a grubby ball, lay a small sock. My breath caught in my throat as I bent down to pick it up.

CHAPTER TWELVE

It could be any child's sock, so why did I feel so sure that it was Jamie's? I stood, gazing down at it in my hand, tears burning. And then I heard the front door open on the floor below. My body tensed. Was it the elderly neighbour coming to see what I was doing—or someone else?

Footsteps began to climb the stairs. Quickly, I stuffed the sock into my pocket. Straining my ears, I could hear each bedroom door open, then close. The steps stopped outside the bathroom and I held my breath, waiting as the door opened.

'Daniel! What are you doing here?'

Standing outside in the gloom of the landing, he stared back at me, disbelievingly. 'I saw your car parked farther down the lane, and guessed . . .'

I interrupted him. 'But that policewoman told me you'd been arrested.' He laughed. 'Then she got it all wrong. Now, tell me what ꭢu're doing here—and how you managed to ꭢ in.'

'That old man with the dog—Gertie—we saw yesterday in the lane. Remember? He had a key. I feel dreadful about conning him though.' I frowned. 'But how did you get in?'

'You didn't shut the front door properly. I saw it ajar and realised this was where you were.' He gave me a searching look. 'Found anything?'

My fingers closed over the little sock in my pocket. Could I trust this man? I shook my head.

'What made you come back to this house?' he said, and his voice changed slightly as he stepped farther into the bathroom.

'I thought Jamie might be here.'

'In Peter Carrick's house? What made you think that?'

The edge of the washbasin pressed into my spine as I moved backwards, away from him.

'You must have a reason. Come on. Out with it.'

His fingers caught hold of my wrist and I winced at their fierceness. 'Daniel! You're hurting me!'

His grip tightened. 'I asked why you thought your son might be in this house. I want an answer. Now!'

Rapping out the last word, he twisted my arm behind my back and I couldn't bite back a groan. How could I once have trusted thi man?

'So I was right about you,' I shouted. 'Y

father-in-law—Peter Carrick—he is part of this drug smuggling. I don't know whether you're working with him, or not, but he's taken Jamie, hasn't he?'

His mouth curled as he laughed. 'How could he? Peter's been in hospital for days.'

'Then it was you!' I sobbed, tears of pain and anger scalding my cheeks. 'How could you do this, Daniel? How could you be so cruel? Tell me what you've done with Jamie?'

I lunged forward, furiously trying to claw his face with my free hand, but my fingers slipped away, catching the collar of his denim shirt, dragging it to one side, revealing a lightly-tanned smooth shoulder.

No healing wounds or fading bruises scarred it.

My gaze slowly lifted to meet the taunting expression in his eyes. This wasn't Daniel Trevose, but his brother Barry.

If he realised I knew, what then? It was like a never-ending nightmare. All I could do was keep up the pretence.

Trying to keep my voice steady, I said, 'Please, let me see Jamie. He'll be so frightened.'

He raised one eyebrow—a mannerism so familiar of Daniel that doubt began to grow in my mind once more. Which brother was this?

But it had to be Barry. The lack of scarring made that certain. Besides, Daniel wouldn't d blackmail notes to himself, would he?

What would be the point? Unless it was to divert suspicion . . .

None of that mattered now. All I wanted was to find my son and know he was safe. 'Two of you would make better bargaining power, I suppose.' The voice was so like Daniel's.

Still gripping my arm, he jerked me away from the washbasin and out of the bathroom, pushing me in front of him to the top of the stairs. For a second, I wondered whether I could lean forward to overbalance him and send him falling to the bottom. Then I realised we both could end up injured and that wouldn't help Jamie at all.

Step by step, he marched me down, kicking my heels when my feet dragged. Once we reached the hall, he guided me out through the immaculate kitchen into the overgrown garden, where the mist had thickened, hiding even the hedges.

Dampness clung to every plant and bush, hanging in large drops of moisture that brushed off as we passed, soaking into my clothes. Even the gulls were silent, but in the distance I could still hear the dull moan of the lighthouse, like a mournful ghost, wailing every few minutes.

A wooden summerhouse loomed up and I almost tripped on its step as I was pushed through the door. It took a moment for eyes to adjust to the darkness inside, befo noticed a heap of plaid blankets piled long reclining garden chair. Under them, one small fist rested above a tangle of fair hair.

'Jamie!'

The closed eyelids fluttered, but didn't open. 'If you've hurt him . . .' The words hissed through my tight lips.

'We need him to sleep, that's all. Anyway, he'll have you for company now.'

My arms were caught and held, something twisted tightly round them, and as I opened my mouth to scream a wodge of cloth was rammed in, stifling any sound.

I lifted my foot to kick out but it was seized and I fell to the floor with a thud, while a length of garden twine tied it to the other one. Trussed like a chicken, unable to move, with tears blinding my eyes, I heard the door close silently and the lock click.

I lay, my body growing colder with each hour that passed, gazing up to where my son lay sleeping. At least I knew he was safe.

A thin ray of sunshine filtered in through the salt encrusted window of the summerhouse and I saw that the mist was clearing. My mouth ached and I could hardly swallow from the cloth filling it. Even contracting and relaxing my muscles wouldn't loosen the twine binding me.

The plaid blankets covering Jamie moved ghtly and I heard the chair creak. His curled opened, fingers stretching out like a star One bare foot dangled, almost touching my face. By moving my head a little, I was able to nudge it with my nose.

He leaned sideways, looking down at me, his blue eyes widening and I saw his mouth smile.

'Mummy!'

Then he frowned, his mouth gathering together. 'Have the baddies caught you?'

I nodded my head and raised my chin, hoping he'd understand and pull out the cloth.

'Matthew says they be very, very bad. Worser than pirates. But he won't let them harm me. Shall I take that handkerchief out of your mouth?'

I nodded rapidly and almost choked as the material was pulled away. 'Oh, Jamie!' I croaked, wanting to hug him. 'Can you undo these bits of string?'

His small fingers tugged at the knots, but they were far too tight and my heartbeat quickened in panic. Someone would come back soon. Then what?

'Matthew says I'd best cut them.' He slid off the long chair and went straight to a shelf of flower pots and balls of green garden twine. Standing on tiptoe, he stretched up and moved his hand along the shelf, scattering bits of earth and dust.

'Here 'tis!'

He held out a pair of secateurs.

'Oh, Jamie,' I said. 'You clever boy!'

It wasn't an easy job for a little boy, but he

109

managed to slide one blade under the twine and finally snap it together, so that the tight binding severed and I was able to pull my wrists apart, rubbing them gently to restore the circulation. Once the feeling had returned, I took the secateurs from him and bent to cut my ankles free.

Now, all we had to do was escape from the summerhouse. The sun had grown much stronger and sunbeams filled the wooden room, quivering in through its dusty window. A window that could be opened. Tugging at the rusty hasp, I managed to heave it outwards a little, but it wasn't wide enough for me to get through.

Lifting Jamie, I pushed him through the gap. 'See if the key's in the door,' I whispered, then heard it turn and the door creak open.

We were free!

Seizing Jamie's hand, I ran across the overgrown lawn, out through the gate and into the lane. All I needed now was the car to start first time.

'Still here?'

The voice from behind made me jump and I swung round to see the elderly neighbour being pulled along by an eager Gertie.

'Find what you were looking for?'

'Yes, thank you,' I said, tugging open the car door and bundling Jamie inside. 'Do your strap up, darling. Quickly.'

I glanced over my shoulder, petrified that

110

we were being followed.

Gertie was sniffing round the front wheels as the engine whirred into life and I had to wait while the old man encouraged her to move, very reluctantly, towards a tree, then raised his hat, stepping back in surprise when the car shot past him, up the lane.

'Are we going home now, Mummy?'

'Yes, darling,' I said, grinding up a gear.

No, I thought, we can't go back to the cottage. It isn't safe any more. So where? It had to be somewhere that neither of the Trevose brothers would find us.

And then I remembered Tim was staying in Falmouth. But, after our meeting together, would he still be there? A hotel by Castle Beach, he said. Putting my foot down hard on the accelerator, I headed in that direction, keeping a careful watch on the rear mirror to make sure no one was following.

The tide was high in Falmouth Bay, washing over rocks and fine sand, when we drove along Cliff Road and parked. With Jamie holding my hand, I enquired at the reception desk of three hotels and was climbing the driveway of a fourth, when the glass doors swung back and Tim walked through.

'Becca?' he said, frowning as he scanned us from head to toe, and I realised how scruffy both Jamie and I must look.

'Can we come in, Tim? Please. It's a long story.'

111

Whether it was the desperate expression on my face, or the fact that Jamie was beginning to cry with tiredness, Tim asked no questions, just guided us back into the hotel and up a wide flight of stairs.

'You look as though you both need a bath. It's through there. I'll have some tea sent up.'

There wasn't much I could do about the state of our clothes, but at least Jamie and I were clean when we went back into Tim's bedroom and found a tray of toasted buns, tea and glass of orange juice on the table.

'Now, are you going to tell me what this is all about, Becca? Have you changed your mind about coming with me?'

I sank down into an armchair, with Jamie cuddled on my lap. For once, the tea was welcome and I drank it quickly, my mouth dry, still tasting of the handkerchief gag.

Tim refilled my cup and sat in the chair opposite, waiting.

'You're not going to believe all this,' I said, brushing crumbs from my jeans.

'Try me,' he replied.

Jamie was fast asleep, wrapped in my arms, by the time I ended the story. Tim had listened, without saying a word.

'Let me get this straight, Becca. The man you rescued from the sea is a drug smuggler? The man you lived with in that cottage? And you still let him stay with you?'

'I didn't think it was true,' I protested.

112

'You put my son at risk, knowing the man was involved in that?'

'Daniel wouldn't hurt Jamie,' I said firmly.

Tim gave a short laugh. 'Oh no! The child's been kidnapped, drugged, and left by himself in a locked shed, Becca. What effect is that going to have on him?'

My teeth bit down on my lower lip. 'I'm sure it wasn't Daniel who kidnapped Jamie.'

'Huh! Just one of his charming friends. What were you thinking of, Becca, letting this villain anywhere near Jamie? Were you so besotted with him?'

'No!'

'So you'll be quite happy to return to Surrey with me in the morning? Start again, where we left off—and forget about everything that's happened, to both you and me?'

He paused, his gaze fixed on me.

'Well, Becca, I'm waiting for an answer.'

What answer could I give Tim? There was no way I could remain in Cornwall. Not after everything that had occurred. It wasn't safe.

As for Daniel . . .

Jamie's warm little body snuggled closer against mine, totally relaxed. How near had I come to losing him? My spine went cold at the thought—if I hadn't found him in Peter Carrick's summerhouse, what might have happened to him?

Just how ruthless was Barry Trevose? E kidnapping a small child was horrific. I c

113

want to imagine what else he might be capable of.

We needed to leave Cornwall as quickly as possible. 'I'll come back to Surrey with you, but we have to leave tonight.'

'So soon? You're exhausted. Both of you need sleep.'

'We can sleep while you drive, Tim.'

'What about your car?'

'It doesn't matter. Leave it here at the hotel. Tell them you'll collect it some other time. Please, Tim. Let's hurry.'

I was carrying Jamie, still fast asleep, down the wide staircase, carefully watching every step to make sure I didn't slip, when someone coming up stopped in front of me, blocking the way. Startled, I raised my eyes and my body froze.

It was the Inspector. 'Well, well, well. You've led us a merry chase, young lady. It's lucky your car was spotted. Shouldn't park on double yellow lines, you know.' He lightly caught my elbow and turned me round.

'Best if we return to your room. Don't want to cause a commotion in reception, do we?'

Wearily, I went back up the stairs. Settling himself into one of the armchairs, he leaned against the cushion and folded his hands into a steeple, resting his plump chin on top of them.

'Now then, my dear, perhaps you'd like to me exactly what you've been up to since gave my policewoman the slip earlier on.

I'm pleased to see your little boy safe and sound. How did you know where to find him? Of course, there is an old saying: "he who hides, can't find". Maybe you know that one?'

'You still think that Daniel and I were in this together, don't you?'

'No,' he said, slowly shaking his head. 'Not with Daniel Trevose.'

I gave a hollow laugh. 'Surely you don't think I'm in league with his brother Barry?'

He scratched his nose. 'Stranger things have happened.'

'It was Barry who kidnapped Jamie.'

'Look, my dear, I can see you don't want to let the little lad out of your sight, so why don't you lay him on the bed and let him sleep in comfort, while you tell me what happened.' He looked across the room to where Tim was sitting by the window. 'Can you ask for a fresh pot of tea to be sent up?'

Like Tim had done earlier, the Inspector let me talk while he listened in silence, before making any comment, then his questions began. 'What made you go to Peter Carrick's house?'

'I don't really know. Some sort of instinct. I just found myself on the road there. And when I thought about it, that house was in such an out of the way spot, it seemed a suitable place to hide Jamie.'

'Did you think Peter Carrick was involved in some way?'

'Well, he and the Trevose brothers knew each other. He bought *The Lady Jane* and the brothers sailed her together. When you arrested Daniel for having drugs on board, it seemed obvious to me that the three of them must be linked.'

'When I arrested Daniel Trevose . . .' The Inspector rubbed one hand across his mouth and for a moment I thought he was smiling behind it. 'He was sailing the boat that night. And we did find narcotics hidden on board the wreck. Therefore Daniel Trevose was smuggling them. An obvious conclusion. More tea?'

He lifted the lid of the pot, poured in hot water and stirred it round with a spoon, before re-filling my cup. 'Unexpected event—that storm. Very lucky you were brave enough to rescue him. And then, of course, his amnesia. Most unfortunate. Really put a spanner in the works, that did.'

'I don't understand,' I said, frowning at him.

Leaning forward, he patted my hand. 'Best not.'

'That's not good enough, Inspector,' I snapped. 'You're forgetting several things, aren't you? I could have drowned, saving Daniel. I let him live in my home, knowing he was a criminal. I was scared out of my wits when the cottage was broken into and those terrifying notes left.

'My child was kidnapped, then I found

myself bound and gagged, locked in a wooden shed, with no idea whether he was alive or dead beside me.

'With the help of my small son, we escaped and then had to drive, panic-stricken in case we were being pursued. And, finally, you appear, like a hobgoblin, turning everything into an unexplained mystery.'

This time, he laughed out loud. 'You're right,' he said, standing up. 'Well, the only fair thing I can do is take you back to the station with me.'

'You're arresting me?'

'Just to give you a few answers, that's all, my dear. Shall we go?'

I shook my head. 'I'm not leaving Jamie.'

Tim moved from where he'd been standing by the window. 'He'll be fine with me, Becca.'

'I'm not leaving him,' I repeated.

Pulling a mobile phone from his pocket, the Inspector stepped outside the bedroom door, returning a minute or two later, to settle into the armchair again.

'Let's ask for another pot of tea while we're waiting.'

'Waiting for what?' I asked.

He raised both eyebrows, his eyes bulging as he twitched his nose. 'The answers.'

Out to sea a light winked, and I remembered the moan of the lighthouse earlier that day. Was it still that same day? So much had happened. All I wanted to do n was sleep, curled up on the bed like my son. To sleep—and forget. But would I ever forget?

The Inspector sat, head back, mouth wide, eyelids closed, making strange grunting noises, a half-eaten chocolate biscuit melting in the saucer of his cup.

Tim stood like a statue by the window, staring out into the growing darkness. I wondered whether his thoughts were the same as mine.

What would our life be, together again? Can love that's been shattered ever re-grow?

Someone tapped on the bedroom door. The Inspector's head jerked sideways, eyes opening, one hand wiping across his mouth. Easing back his shoulders, he rose stiffly from the chair and walked to the door.

When it opened, Daniel came in. Or is it Barry, I thought, my heartbeat racing, until he smiled.

'Daniel?'

I looked questioningly at the Inspector.

'Just listen,' he said, settling down into the armchair again. 'To a tale of two brothers. Almost identical in appearance, but totally unalike in character. Brother One enjoys a lifestyle way above his income, so he gambles, and loses, and loses, and goes on losing, until he's deeply in debt to all the wrong people.

'Brother Two has a boat and quite often ☐ils over to France and other parts of the ☐st, and sometimes Brother One goes with

118

him. Ah, say the wrong people, we know a way you can repay all you owe us, yet have plenty left over for yourself.

'So Brother One does exactly what they tell him, when he and Brother Two go sailing together, until one day Brother Two discovers how his boat is being used.

'However, he wants to know who is making Brother One do these wicked things, so he goes to the police and suggests they keep a careful watch on his boat next voyage to discover who receives the goodies.

'Now there's another old saying you may have heard: "It never does to plan" and unfortunately, two things happened on that voyage. First, Brother One stayed all night gambling and drinking, and missed the tide, so Brother Two, foolishly as it turned out, decided to make the journey alone and see who was waiting the other side. Secondly, a terrific storm drove the boat on to the rocks, wrecking it.

'Brother Two was thankfully saved from drowning—and I think you know the rest of the story, my dear.'

I looked across at Daniel. 'You were working with the police?'

'Once my memory returned properly, yes. They knew exactly who I was, right from the start, but were so close to catching those behind the drug smuggling, they kept up the pretence.'

119

'And I was pig in the middle!'

'I'm really sorry, Becca. I wanted so much to tell you, but the Inspector here warned me against it. Safer to keep you in the dark. Not that it turned out that way though.'

The Inspector pushed back his chair and stood up. 'Everything's been cleared up, nice and tidy now and we've the whole bunch safely in custody. That's all you need to know.'

'Was Peter Carrick involved?' I asked.

He shook his head. 'Only his house—while he was out of the way, in hospital. Barry Trevose, pretending to be Daniel, visited him and collected the key. Probably already planning to take your little lad there.'

I shivered, and Daniel's hand closed over mine, squeezing my fingers. 'It's ended now, Becca.'

'I really did think you were involved, Daniel.'

'I know you did, and I hated living a lie. Every accusation you made, was so right. And when Jamie was taken . . . The Inspector had to forcibly take me away, to prevent me telling you everything there and then.'

'So you weren't arrested?'

I leaned my forehead against his. 'Are we still leaving tonight, or waiting until the morning now?'

I'd forgotten Tim and quickly stepped away ɔm Daniel as he came across the room ⱱards us.

120

'You're going with him, Becca?' Daniel's blue eyes were filled with dismay. 'I thought . . .'

Tim laughed. 'Of course she's coming with me!

'D'you think she'd want to stay here? With you? No way!'

They faced each other, backs straight, jaws thrust out, like two fighters waiting for the bell. Daniel, I noticed, was an inch or two taller.

On the bed, Jamie stretched both arms above his head and yawned, then sat up, smiling. 'Matthew says it be time to go home— and Daniel be coming with us.'

Matthew says . . .

Daniel turned to look at me, one eyebrow raised in question, and I held out my hands, taking his and Jamie's.

'Becca!'

'I'm sorry, Tim.'

It was late that summer, on a warm September day, when Daniel and I made our vows in the tiny village church, where a polished brass plaque is set into one of its thick stone walls.

In Memory of Matthew Poldhu
Born 15 May 1735
Who gave his life
saving his brother from the sea
6 July 1750

Each time I read those words, I wonder,

could it be . . .

Down by the water's edge, I can see Jamie, paddling through small rock pools left by the tide. Every so often he stops, crouching down on his heels and peers into the shallow water, trailing his fingers.

I watch his fair head turn sideways, then nod, as he talks. But not to an imaginary friend any more.

Daniel is there, beside him. Jamie's best friend—and mine now, forever.